Deep Wheel Orcadia

HARRY JOSEPHINE GILES is a writer and performer
from Orkney, living in Edinburgh. Their collection *Tonguit* was
shortlisted for the Forward Prize for Best First Collection, and
The Games for the Edwin Morgan Poetry Award and Saltire
Prize for Best Collection. Working across poetry, theatre and
games, they were the 2009 BBC Scotland slam champion,
and have performed globally from New York's
Bowery Poetry to Romania's Teszt and the
New Zealand Writers Festival.

Also by Harry Josephine Giles

Tonguit

The Games

Deep Wheel Orcadia

HARRY JOSEPHINE GILES

PICADOR POETRY

First published in the UK 2021 by Picador
an imprint of Pan Macmillan
The Smithson, 6 Briset Street, London EC1M 5NR
EU representative: Macmillan Publishers Ireland Ltd, 1st Floor
The Liffey Trust Centre, 117–126 Sheriff Street Upper, Dublin 1, D01 YC43
Associated companies throughout the world
www.panmacmillan.com

ISBN 978-1-5290-6660-9

5 7 9 8 6

A CIP catalogue record for this book is available from the British Library.

Printed and bound by CPI Group (UK) Ltd, Croydon, CR0 4YY

MIX
Paper | Supporting
responsible forestry
FSC® C116313

Visit **www.picador.com** to read more about all our books
and to buy them. You will also find features, author interviews and
news of any author events, and you can sign up for e-newsletters
so that you're always first to hear about our new releases.

Taeble o Contents

Twa

Tree

The Fock

ASTRID, a artist, comed haem tae Orcadia
INGA, her mither, captain o a lighteen yole
ØYVIND, Astrid's faither, a maet tekniecian
DARLING, a visietor fae Mars
NOOR, a xeno-arkaeolojist
EYNAR, a steward o the Hoose
OLAF, a lighter wi Inga
HIGGIE, a sisadmin at the Light refinery
MARGIT, a lighter wi her awn yole
BRENNA, a young radiecal
GUNNIE, a junior tekniecian, an bairn o Margit
Ither Orcadians: ASLAUG, AUGA, DAGMAR, ERIKA,
ERLEND, INGRID, KARI, SIGURD, TORSTEN, UNN,
an plenty more, an thir bairns.

The People

ASTRID, an artist, come home to Orcadia
INGA, her mother, captain of a lighting boat
ØYVIND, Astrid's father, a foodmeat technician
DARLING, a visitor from Mars
NOOR, a xeno-archaeologist
EYNAR, a landlord of the local bar
OLAF, a lighter with Inga
HIGGIE, a systems administrator at the Light refinery
MARGIT, a lighter with her own boat
BRENNA, a young radical
GUNNIE, a junior technician, and Margit's child
Other Orcadians: ASLAUG, AUGA, DAGMAR, ERIKA, ERLEND, INGRID,
KARI, SIGURD, TORSTEN, UNN, and many more, and their children.

Wan

Astrid docks

The chime o the tannoy is whit taks her back,
fer hid isno chaenged, nae more as the wirds
summonan her tae the airlock: her wirds,
at sheu isno heard fer eyght geud year.

Sheu waatched the Deep Wheel approch, gray-green,
hids Central Staetion tirlan yet
anent the yallo yotun, peedie
bolas teddert aroon hids ring,

pierheids trang wi yoles, wi glims,
an fund the gloup atween ootbye an in
clossan slaa – but only noo,
wi this soond, deus sheu ken whar sheu is.

Astrid docks

The chime of the tannoy is what brings her back, because it hasn't
changed, and neither have the words summoning her to the airlock: her
words, which she hasn't heard for eight goodlong years.

She watched the Deep Wheel approach, grey-green, its Central Station
still turntwistwhirlspinning againstaboutbefore the yellow gas giant, little
bolas ropemoormarried around its ring

pierheads fullactiveintimate with boats, with gleampointlights, and
found the chasmcleft between outside and inside closing laxslowly – but
only now, with this sound, does she know where she is.

Sheu leuks aroon the ither fock,
tryan tae mynd wha's uncan, an wha's
whas bairn, an wha's gien a naem fae sheu left,
an whas naem sheu shoud mynd yet.

An Astrid leuks tae anither body,
stannan at the vizzie-screen:
taall, pael, reid hair ravsie,
Martian style, gappan at the sight.

Sheu coud been a student fae college, but no
like Astrid, at waants tae waatch her an kinno
disno: sheu's ferfil bonnie an warld-like
fer Mars, but here i'the ramse poly

habitats o inner space,
sheu's a aafil queerie sowl.
The visietor leuks aroon an grins
at Astrid, at leuks awey, no kennan

  She looks around the other folk, trying to rememberknowreflectwill
who is strangerweird, and who is whose child, and who's taken a name
since she left, and whose name she should still rememberknowreflectwill.
  And Astrid looks at another personbody, standing at the viewing
screen: tall, pale, red hair roughabundantunkempt in a Martian style,
gapingfoolishmindless at the sight.
  She could have been a student from college, but not like Astrid,
who wants to watch and also doesn't: she's veryfearfully finepretty and
healthynormal for Mars, but here in the roughcurtbitter plasticpolymer
  habitats of inner space, she's a veryawfully strangequeer soulperson.
The visitor looks around and grinyearns at Astrid, who looks away, not
knowing

whit wey tae meet incoman joy.
The jaas o the transport appen, a gant
thrumman the bonns o the ship, a kord
whan the gangwey connecks. Astrid's taen

a peedie an weyghty life on her back,
an whan sheu steps intae the airlock
sheu catches the grief o whit will come
if the pairts o her canno find thir piece.

whathowwherewhy to meet incoming joy. The jaws of her transport
open, a yawngasp thrumming the bones of the ship, a chord when the
gangway connects. Astrid's brought
a little and heavymeaningful life on her back, and when she steps into
the airlock, she begins to feel grief about what will happen if the parts of
her can't find their placedistancepartwhile.

Inga Lighter an Øyvind Grower waatch Astrid come in

Inga is thinkan, whit wey tae explaen
the staetion noo? That scant the lighteen,

that scrimp the tithes. Øyvind is fashan
at whither or no her vooels'll come haem.

Inga rubs her clippert heid
an thinks: Varday is tint the haalage,

Aikeray the traed, an only
the kirk is ivver fill, fer prayan.

Øyvind birls a pod in his lang
fingers an waatches the ship link

Inga the Lighter and Øyvind the Grower watch Astrid come in
Inga is thinking about whathowwherewhy to explain what the station
is like now. So scarceshortsmall the lighting,
so meagrestunted the tithes. Øyvind is fussvexworrying about whether
or not her vowels will come home.
Inga rubs her shorn head and thinks: Varday has losemissfailed the
haulage,
Aikeray the trade, and only the church is ever full, for praying.
Øyvind whirlrushdancespins a pod in his long fingers and watches the
ship glidetrotrestconnect

intae Meginwick's muckle dock,
a cathedral o girders an stances appenan

intae the haaf. Inga coonts
the yoles. Øyvind mynds on his years

on the Mars–Orcadia shippeen reute
an whit he kens o surface life,

whit he can share noo wi his dowter.
An whan the airlock appens an Astrid

is eyght year aalder an jeust the sam,
her spacer fock is waitan, still.

Øyvind shifts an appens his airms.
Inga says, "Buddo," an lifts her bags.

    into Meginwick's greatbig dock, a cathedral of girders and
platformsites opening
    into deep space. Inga counts the boats. Øyvind
rememberknowreflectwills his years
    on the Mars–Orcadia shipping route and what he knows of planetary
life,
    what he can share now with his daughter. And when the airlock opens
and Astrid
    is eight years older and just the same, her spacer folk are waiting,
stillfixedsecretsilent.
    Øyvind changedodgemoves and opens his arms. Inga says,
"FriendChildLove," and lifts her bags.

The visietor, Darling, leuks fer a piece tae bide

"J-Just to look," sheu says, catchan the poynt
o the yolewife's quaistion. Sheu wis been raedan aboot
the Wrack-Hofn's mistry, aboot the yoles
landan thir haal o Lights, aboot the stoor
i'the gowden tide, aboot the paece o distance,

aboot a uncan wey o spaekan, o wirkan,
o pittan up wirds, o bidan, belongan, an waantid
tae leuk. But noo sheu's speiran the first body
sheu saa i'the bay fer the first directions, an habbers,
fer the first time no kennan hoo tae explaen hersel.

The visitor, Darling, looks for a placedistancepartwhile to waitstaylive

"Just to look," she says, catching the point of the boat worker's question. She has been reading about the Wreck-Havenharbour's mystery, about the boats landing their haulcatch of Lights, about the stormstrifestrainspeeddust in the golden seatimetide, about the peace of distance,

about a strangerweird way of speaking, of working, of praying, of waitstayliving, belonging, and wanted to look. But now she's asking the first personbody she saw in the hangar for the first directions, and stammers, for the first time not knowing how to explain herself.

"Ir ye?" says the wife, no askan. A din-faced
stuggie body, her snackie haands is deep
i'the wires o her craft. "Ye'll waant tae spaek tae Eynar
o the Hoose. Whit ye'd caa wir *bar*. He'll sort ye.
Tell him Margit sent ye." Like Eynar, Margit

kens the guff o traed. Sheu poynts the wey.
Darling's waatchan the fock on the pier fae the transport –
twa aalder fock tae meet yin ither lass,
at disno seem tae ken whar sheu's comed an aa –
an Margit waatches wha hid is haads whas ee.

"Thir," sheu says, an looder again, "That wey."
Darling tries tae gaither Martian manners.
"Thank you so so much," says Darling. "I'm Darling."
Anither first: sheu blushes, seean Margit's
edge o a smirk an hearan Margit's "Ir thoo."

"Is that so?" says the woman, not asking. A sallow shorttoughbutch
personbody, her cleverquicksharp hands are deep in the wires of her craft.
"You should speak to Eynar at the House. It's what you'd call our bar. He'll
help. Tell him Margit sent you." Like Eynar, Margit
knows the stinkpuffsnortnonsense of trade. She points the way.
Darling's watching the folk on the pier from the transport – two older
folk to meet that other girlwoman, who doesn't seem to know where she's
come either – and Margit watches who is holding whose eye.
"There," she says, and louder again, "That way." Darling tries to gather
Martian manners. "Thank you so so much," says Darling. "I'm Darling."
Another first: she blushes, seeing Margit's edge of a smile and hearing
Margit's "Is that so."

Astrid an Darling settle in

Astrid aets wi her fock. "Thoo'll wirk?"
speirs Inga ower the protein soup.
"A'm here tae draa," says Astrid. "Tae wirk
at me art. A'm needan ideas fae haem."

"Yass," says Inga, "grand that. Thoo'll tak
a job or twa fae the rotas forbye."
Øyvind touches Astrid's airm.
"Hid's grand thoo're haem. Thir plenty time."

Halfweys roond the staetion, Darling,
breeksed wi sailan, pangit wi hopp,
sits i'the Hoose wi a plaet o maet.
Eynar teuk it tae her, sportan

Astrid and Darling settle in

Astrid eats with her folk. "Will you work?" asks Inga over the protein soup. "I'm here to draw," says Astrid. "To work on my art. I wantneed ideas from home."

"Yes," says Inga, "that's goodbig. And you'll take a job or two from the rotas as well." Øyvind touches Astrid's arm. "It's goodbig that you're home. There's plenty of time."

Halfway around the station, Darling, knackered from sailing, fullbursting with hope, sits in the House with a plate of foodmeat. Eynar brought it to her, sporting

a apron an a smile. Sheu tryd
tae speir him aboot his fock an the staetion:
he nodded an brustled back tae the bar.
Sheu waatches the fock an aets her maet.

Astrid spaeks aboot the journey,
aboot whit her pals in Mars is deuan.
The wirds is lood in thir peedie quaaters.
Inga an Øyvind's speuns rudge.

Darling notts a plan on her slaet
o whit sheu waants tae see; she hopps
a smoosie body will ask whit sheu's deuan.
Naebody deus. Sheu dights her plaet.

Eftir, the both o thaim lie i thir bunks
on conter airms o the Wheel, birlan,
askin thirsels if thir maed a mistaek,
askin thirsels whit wey is a haem.

 an apron and a smile. She tried to ask him about his people and
the station: he nodded and bustlecrackled back to the bar. She watched the
people and ate her foodmeat.
 Astrid speaks about the journey, about what her friends on Mars are
doing. The words are loud in their little rooms. Inga and Øyvind's spoons
gratehackrattle.
 Darling notes down a plan on her slate of what she wants to see;
she hopes a nosy personbody will ask what she's doing. Nobody does.
She cleanwipes her plate.
 Later, both of them lie in their bedbunks on oppositeopposing arms
of the Wheel, whirlrushdancespinning, asking themselves if they've made
a mistake, asking themselves whathowwherewhy a home is.

Olaf Lighter an Eynar o the Hoose speir at the new teknolojy

"Whit wey deus hid wirk?" asks Eynar, pooran
a beer. "A'm no sure," says Olaf,
"but yin arkaeolojist, ken, ach,
whit's her naem, telt hid like this—"

The jimpit yoleman taks twa glesses
an a pock o nuts an steers
this subtle injines trou the warp
o time, noo rings o spirit on

the binkled aluminium bar.
"The drive maks a pock, see,
o hyperspace tae win trou,
tae exceed relatievistic constraints."

Olaf the Lighter and Eynar the Landlord question the new technology

"Whathowwherewhy does it work?" asks Eynar, pouring a beer.
"I'm not sure," says Olaf, "but that archaeologist, oh, you know, what's her
name, told me it was like this—"

The smallslenderneatdainty boat worker takes two empty glasses and
a packetpocket of nuts and steers these subtle engines through the warp of
time, now rings of spirit on

the bentdented aluminium bar. "The drive makes a packetpocket,
see, of hyperspace to reachtravelachieve through, to exceed relativistic
constraints."

"Ya, but," says Eynar, "I thowt hid wis
more ontolojiecal restrictions
as teknolojiecal limits. Whit wey
ir thay avoydan catastrophic

temporal paradox, eh?" Olaf
taks a drowt o his ael an says,
"Ya weel. Best kens. An best kens
thay maan, fer hid's bad enogh tae loss

the laast bit o the laast bit
o wir shippeen ithoot messan wi fuckan
multiversal anomalies
an aa." An Eynar, no drinkan, says,

"A'll drink tae yin," lukkan ower
the empty poly chairs an taebles,
Olaf's grayan hair, an weyghan
the wirth o his bisness, the size o his saeveens,

"Yes, but," says Eynar, "I thought the problem was more ontological
restrictions than technological limits. Whathowwherewhy can they avoid
catastrophic
temporal paradox, eh?" Olaf takes a draught of his beer and says,
"Yes well. Gods know. And gods know they must because it's bad enough
to lose
the last bit of the last bit of our shipping without messing with fucking
multiversal anomalies as well." And Eynar, not drinking, says,
"I'll drink to that," looking over the empty plasticpolymer chairs and
tables, Olaf's greying hair, and weighing the worth of his business, the size
of his savings,

the price o a ticket tae Ross or Mars
or Proxima Centauri Twa,
an runnan the nummers again, an wipan
the trails o the hyperdrive fae the bar.

the price of a ticket to Ross or Mars or Proxima Centauri B, and
running the numbers again, and wiping the trails of the hyperdrive from
the bar.

Higgie the Codd at her screens

Aence sheu wis a packer: whan the Lights cam in
sheu wirked the spectral refractors, prismatic acceleraetors,
containment dykes, brissan somtheen skare an lowse
intae somtheen birnable. No a coorse wark –
buttons an levers, mosstleens – sheu jeust needed care
an the canny gy o timeen. But sheu an her pals wis aye
tae loss the unavoydable race wi aatomaetion.
Higgie wis lucky: sheu wis keepid on at the skeul
tae ken the maths tae tak the coarse tae qualiefy
fer maintenance, so sheu wis the body lukkan eftir
machines lukkan eftir Lights, an than the body
lukkan eftir machines lukkan eftir machines.

Higgie the Coder at her screens

Once she was a packer: when the Lights came in, she worked the
spectral refractors, prismatic accelerators, containment wallfieldbarriers,
squeezepressbruising something clearbrightcut and loosefree into
something burnable. It wasn't roughhardnasty work – buttons and
levers, mostly – she just needed care and the skilledwisemagicalcautious
sensecompetence of timing. But she and her friends were always going to
lose the unavoidable race with automation. Higgie was luckyblessedhappy:
she'd stayed at school to know the maths to take the course to qualify for
maintenance, so she was the personbody looking after machines looking
after Lights, and then the personbody looking after machines looking after
machines.

Thir aalder noo, an only Higgie bade tae be
a elder. Dagmar's maed a faimly on Wolf; Kari
teuk a Martian job in maet; Torsten deed
an naen o them ivver spaek aboot hid; Higgie, back
croppenan more wi ivry year, dellt wi codd
an solder intae machines, missan the clashan, thinkan
in script an circuit. Sheu monietors: here at the plant,
by screen, an eftir, i'the back pew o the kirk. Sheu maks
peedie adjustments: wha sits whar, whit wirds is needed,
whan tae apply comfort an whan tae chide or spaek
a truth. Sheu isno alaen. She kens sheu disno sing
in tune, but at the plant an wi her screens sheu sings.

They're older now, and only Higgie waitstaylived to be an elder.
Dagmar made a family on Wolf; Kari took a Martian job in foodmeat;
Torsten died, and none of them ever speak about it; Higgie, back
bendcramptwisting more with every year, delved with code and solder into
machines, missing the noisegossip, thinking in codeprogramscripture and
circuit. She monitors: here at the plant, by screen, and after, in the back
pew of the kirk. She makes little adjustments: who sits where, what words
are needed, when to apply comfort and when to chide or speak a truth.
She is not alone. She knows she does not sing in tune, but at the plant and
with her screens she sings.

Astrid sketches Orcadia

Sheu trails a finger ower her slaet i'the curve
o her planet, than wi a canny swirl bleums
hids swaalls o yallo an corkalit. Wi shairp
stroks, the airms o Central Staetion skoot
atwart the screen, an peedie tigs an picks
mairk oot the eydent piers o Meginwick
i'the corner o her careful composietion.

An lukkan oot the peedie vizzie-bell,
doon the taing o Hellay, airm o the kirk,
the dammer o the Deep Wheel surroondan her,
Astrid feels hersel faa, an lift, an faa.
Liv oot, sheu dights the natralism fae
her slaet, an stairts ower again, abstrack,
wi only the nirt o the thowt o coman haem

Astrid sketches Orcadia

She trails a finger over her slate in the curve of her planet, then with a skilledwisemagicalcautious swirl blooms its swellwaves of yellow and scarlet dye. With sharp strokes, the arms of Central Station jutthrust acrossover the screen, and little taptwitchteases and tapchaptakes mark out the constantindustrious piers of Meginwick in the corner of her careful composition.

And looking out of the little viewsurveystudyaiming-bubblebell, down the promontory of Hellay, arm of the church, the shockstunconfusion of the Deep Wheel surrounding her, Astrid feels herself fall, and lift, and fall. Palm flat, she cleanwipes the naturalism from her slate, and begins again, abstract, with only the crumbknot of the thought of coming home

an odd gittan seean that peedie odds:
black lines fer the starns, blue dubs
fer the tides, green aircs fer the grand skail
o wheels an airms an bolas gaithered roond Central.
Mindan her lessons fae college, sheu follows sense
intae shape, an shape intae color, an noo sheu's closser
tae the grace ootbye, but closser maks more o a ranyie.

Again her dightan liv. Again a blenk.
Astrid steeks her een an haads the device
tae her chest, sam as her braethan wir liftan Orcadia
tae the surface. But the screen bides skarpy,
an the view bides stamagastan, an Astrid
settles back tae waatch an braethe an mynd,
her fingers restan jeust abeun the slaet.

and growing strangedifferent from seeing so little difference. Black
lines for the stars, blue poolpuddlemuds for the seatimetides, green arcs
for the goodbig scatterspreadspill of wheels and arms and bolas gathered
round Central. Rememberknowreflectwilling her lessons from college, she
follows sense into shape, and shape into colour, and now she's closer to the
graceglory outside, but closer makes more of a writhingpain.

Again her cleanwiping palm. Again a blankblink. Astrid shutdarkens
her eyes and holds the device to her chest, as if breathing was lifting
Orcadia to the surface. But the screen waitstaylives barethinbarren, and
the view waitstaylives bewildershockoverwhelming, so Astrid settles back
to watch and breathe and rememberknowreflectwill, her fingers resting
just above the slate.

The pieces Darling's been

Fer her coman o age she asked o her faithers
a week's resiedential on Aald Eart.
Nae Ball, nae press confrence, nae giftid
Executiveship, nae ship, even,
tho aa her brithers wis taen the sleekest
o sublight racers. Thay naeraboot
imploded, but sheu wis inherieted airts
an negotiated the week as traed
fer a simmer wirkan at senior manajment.
Mars simmers is ower lang.

The placesdistancepartwhiles Darling's been

For her coming of age she asked from her fathers a week's residential
on Old Earth. No Ball, no press conference, no gifted Executiveship,
no ship, even, though all of her brothers had taken the sleekest in
sublightspeed racers. They almost imploded, but she had inherited
skilldirectiongrift and negotiated the week in return for a summer
working in senior management. Mars summers are very long.

That wis the stairt o her travaigan.
Foo wi the guff o fifty square mile
o aald equatorial rainforest, no
landscaepid ava, sheu kent
sheu wadno gang haem, but see as gret
a lot o the seiven starns as sheu coud.
Sheu peyed a ecogaird tae mairk her
on the wrang manifest, an fleed. Sheu saa
the Natralist munka-hooses on Phobos,
whar papar refused ony maet traeted

This was the start of her roamingramblingtravels. Drunkmadfull on the stinkpuffsnortnonsense of fifty square miles of old equatorial rainforest, not landscaped at all, she knew she wouldn't go home, but see as much of the seven stars as she could. She paid an environmental quarantine agent to mark her down on the wrong manifest, and flew. She saw the Naturalist monasteries on Phobos, where holies refused any foodmeat treated

wi more as fire, praeched wershy beauty.
Sheu saa a demonstraetion staetion
o sepratist Angles: bred, snod,
rich, blond, an weel-airmed.
Her faithers' credited wirds – first barman,
than teely, than dortan – trackid her
fae Europan federal mines tae stentless
pairties orbitan Wolf. Thay wir even
bowt bulletin time on the ansible network.
At lang an at lent sheu tint thir trackers

with more than fire, preached thinwatery beauty. She saw
a demonstration station of separatist Angles: trainbreddrilled,
cleantrimabsolute, rich, blond, and well-armed. Her fathers'
moneyrespected words – first ragefrothseething, then pleadwheedling,
then sulkforsaking – tracked her from federal mines on Europa to
unrestrainedendless parties orbiting Wolf. They had even bought time for
a bulletin on the ansible network. At long last and after much effort she
lost their trackers

on the unregistered Autonomist traeder
whar, awey, sheu teuk her new naem
an body an face, whar sheu teuk time
tae cheuss an recover, at teuk her here
tae Orcadia, the innermosst Nordren staetion,
aence the edge, aence the centre,
pangit an empty yet, wi Darling,
eftir peyan her rodd ower that
grand a piece o space, lukkan
fer a peedie piece tae listen an leuk.

on the unregistered Autonomist trader where, awaydeaddistracted, she took her new name and body and face, where she took time to choose and recover, which took her here to Orcadia, the Northern station closest to the galactic centre, once the edge, once the centre, fullbursting and empty still, with Darling, after buypaying her way across such a goodbig placedistancepartwhile of space, looking for a little placedistancepartwhile to listen and look.

Inga an Olaf at the lighteen

Inga's at the helm, waatchan
fer lowes, fer shifts i'the drifts o rouk;
Olaf the sightsman's at the daikles,
airtan oot a trail o Lights
   tae a dinger, a haal.

The linecrew is raedy. A fair while fae
a geud landeen. The wind o the yotun
is sma the day: cheust a hunner
metres a second. The yole chirps
   fae the gowd whips.

Inga and Olaf at the lighting
 Inga is at the helm, watching for flameglowflickerflares, for shifts in the drifts of fogfrost; Olaf, the screen monitor, is at the compasses, trying to find a trail of Light to a strike, a haulcatch.
 The linecrew are ready. It's been a long time since a good landing. The wind of the gas giant is low today: just a hundred metres per second. The boat creakraspcomplains from the golden gustdarttwistattacks.

Sailan as quiet an present here
as a meditaetion o Phobos papar,
thay wirk the wark the staetion wis biggid
tae wirk, hintan the fuel at fuels,
            the oyl at oyls

a interstellar system o industry,
traed, galactic expansion: Light.
Inga an Olaf is aye a kord
wi voltage differs, atmospheric
            jabble, mairjins.

Olaf spys a peak an mairks hid.
Inga senses a chaenge i'the paitren
o his concentraetion, an waits.
Thir notheen tae deu but wait.
            His een spairk.

Sailing as quiet and present here as a meditation of Phobos holies,
they work the work that the station was built to do, gathergleansnatching
the fuel that fuels, the oil that oils
    an interstellar system of industry, trade, galactic expansion: Light.
Inga and Olaf are always a chord with voltage differentials, atmospheric
ripplesagitationconfusionchoppiness, margins.
    Olaf spots a peak and marks it. Inga senses a change in the pattern
of his concentration, and waits. There is nothing to do but wait. His eyes
spark.

He checks his chairter anent his ladar
anent his osc, turns – an thay see hid
black horn brakkan gowd,
hulk looman ower the yole.
                    "Wrack! Brace!"

Inga rives the yole tae,
the linecrew an Olaf stellt tae thir bars,
the waa atween the crew an daeth
gaen flinterkin. The hurlan pulse
                    o thir reid alairm.

But—the yole—pulls clear!— skewan
anunder the whalman dairk o the wrack.
Ivry lighter gies a bustan
braeth, an settles sam as this
                    wir ordinar.

He checks his mapper againstaboutbefore his laser radar
againstaboutbefore his oscilloscope, turns – and they see it: black prow
breaking gold, hulk looming over the boat. "Wreck! Brace!"
     Inga wrenchripbreaks the boat away, the linecrew and Olaf fixbraced to
their bars, the wall between the crew and death gone flimsygaudyfrivolous.
The speedthrowrolldriving pulse of their red alarm.
     But—the boat—pulls clear!— twistskewshunning under the
overwhelming dark of the wreck. Every lighter gives a burstescaping
breath, and settles as if this were ordinary.

The wrack's anither gret baest,
the second this crew is fund, o plenty
fund by the staetion, an more the laast
twatree year. A killer, a mistry,
an noo a godssend.

Fer a wrack like this will win a boonty.
Hid isno a haal o Lights, but
thir fock at pey fer this things noo.
Whan Inga relays thir stance, hid credits
anither survival.

The wreck's another great animalmonster, the second this crew has found, of the many found by the station, and more the last few years. A killer, a mystery, and now a salvagewrecktreasure.

Because a wreck like this will reachtravelachieve a bounty. It isn't a haulcatch of Lights, but there are people who pay for these things now. As Inga transmits their co-ordinates, it credits another survival.

Øyvind Astridsfaither, wirkan

The pinchers, maet
an spoot is only
visible trou

a microscopp,
but tae Øyvind
hid's like he's haalan

a ship: his muscles
is haaden in that
tight a tension.

Brenna an Gunnie,
young eens rotad
tae wirk wi him,

Øyvind, Astrid's father, at work
The tongs, foodmeat and syringespout are only visible through
a microscope but to Øyvind it's like he's hauling
a ship: his muscles are held in such a tight tension.
Brenna and Gunnie, young ones assigned to work with him,

is cheetran i'the corner.
He glowers an lays
the braeth-thick

shaef o protein
intae hids piece,
than shifts tae the next.

"Smell yin," he says.
Øyvind glories
i'the guff o the lab.

"Only haand-
growen reeks
this geud."

Brenna comes
aside him, asks,
"Disno nano-

    are chucklegiggling in the corner. He scowlstares and putlaystillweaves
the breath-thick
    slice of protein into its placedistancepartwhile, then shifts to the next.
    "Smell that," he says. Øyvind glories in the stinkpuffsnortnonsense of
the lab.
    "Only the hand-cultivated stinksmokes this good."
    Brenna comes beside him, asks, "Doesn't nano-

replicaetion
smell the sam?"
"Wheesht," he says.

He's takkan a coarse:
communiecaetions.
He kens his rowes

o protein dishes
maan rebrand
as luxury.

His airms birn.
His een tift.
He growes shairper.

replication smell the same?" "Quiet," he says.
He's taking a course: communications. He knows his rows
of protein dishes must rebrand as luxury.
His arms burn. His eyes throbfester. He grows sharper.

The arkaeolojist at the Wrack-Hofn

Noor steers her skiff trou the voyd hulks.
Hid's been a langersome day, the trachle o loggan
ivry mett o the wrack, Inga's godssend.

Fae sheu's comed tae space sheu's fund her body
thickenan – Orcadia's gravitaetional spin
a drag on her meun-growen bonns – an mynd thinnan.

Aence sheu wis yivver tae set her diastimeter
on the deck o a cell. Sheu'd sneck the laser
an dirl wi the new nummers: the thowt o paitrens

i'the teum plans o this gret black reums,
i'the shairp angles o thir slite black waas,
somepiece a staen tae mak thaim intae meanan.

The archaeologist at the Wreck-Havenharbour

Noor steers her skiff through the emptyabandoned hulks. It has been a
longtiring day, the drudgemuddletrudge of logging every measuremarklot
of the wreck, Inga's salvagewrecktreasure.

Since she came to space she's found her body thickening – Orcadia's
gravitational spin a drag on her moon-grown bones – and her mind thinning.

Once she was eagershakeanxious to set her distance-measurer on the
floor of a chamber. She'd switch on the laser and thrillpierceshakewhirl to
the new numbers: the thought of patterns

in the emptyhungry plans of these great black rooms, in the sharp
angles of their smoothstilllevel black walls, somewhere a stone to make
them into meaning.

Noo ivry twatree Stannart Month the lighters
tak anither wrack wi raedeens tae mirk
anither theory. The waas she passes is silent,

rich wi unanswerability: ships or staetions
or sculptures or temples or byres – sheu speeds the skiff –
or tombs or warks – speeds faaster yet – or follies

or calculaetors or classreum exercises
o Arkieteck-Gods. Nae drive, nae rudder, nae hairt,
nae braens, nae lungs, nae hass, nae tong, nae will,

undeeman abeun her, undeeman anunder, bund
in orbit ahint the Deep Wheel, the Hofn
aye growan in grandur an skrinklan in sense.

Now every few Standard Months the lighters bring another wreck with
readings to obscuredulldarken another theory. The walls she passes are
silent,
    rich with unanswerability: ships or stations or sculptures or temples
or barns – she speeds the skiff – or tombs or factories – speeds faster still
– or follies
    or calculators or classroom exercises of Architect-Gods. No drive, no
rudder, no heart, no brain, no lungs, no throatneckpass, no tongue, no will,
    enormousintenseunbelievable above her, enormousintenseunbelievable
below her, bound in orbit behind the Deep Wheel, the Havenharbour
always growing in grandeur and shrinkdying in sense.

Astrid gangs tae kirk

"Thoo'll come?" asks Øyvind, aesy enogh,
so Astrid sayed her "Yass" afore
myndan sheu wis faithless noo.
Sheu cam an fund sheu kent the wirds

tae ivry sang, an hoo tae speir
this god fer saefty an yin fer maet,
anither fer wittans an feck. Awey,
sheu telt Orcadia's past tae the grunders:

the curn o fock fae a curn o ships
at cam to big a curn o a staetion
an raffled thir myndeen o some histry
intae a kinno culture, parteeclar.

Astrid goes to church

"Will you come?" asked Øyvind, casually enough, so Astrid said her
"Yes" before rememberknowreflectwilling she was faithless now. She came
and found she knew the words

to every song, and how to ask this god for safety and that for foodmeat
and another for wisdomknowledgenews and powerworthattention.
Awaydeaddistracted, she told Orcadia's past to the planet-dwelling people:

the fewsmallgrain people from a fewsmallgrain ships that came to build
a fewsmallgrain station, and tanglemuddled their giftremembrancememory
of strangespecial history into a sort of culture, specificstrange.

Here, sheu didno think o the differ
atween tael an true. Awey,
sheu lairned tae be a aafil cynic.
Here, sheu coonts the ruives i'the reuf

trou the lang an weel-kent sermon.
An Higgie's soprano cracks the sam
notts ahint her, an wi this truth
Astrid finds forgieness: a caald

waarmth at's notheen tae deu wi belief
an aatheen tae deu wi haird pews,
thin yarns, gray beuks,
an so is a myndeen tae her fae the gods.

    Here, she didn't think of the difference between tale and true.
Awaydeaddistracted, she learned to be an awful cynic. Here, she counts
the rivets in the roof
    through the long and familiar sermon. And Higgie's soprano cracks the
same notes behind her, and in this truth Astrid finds forgiveness: a cold
    warmth that has nothing to do with belief and everything to do with hard
pews, thin stories, grey books, and as such is a giftremembrancememory to
her from the gods.

Darling gangs tae view the wracks

Sheu thowt thir'd be somtheen more,
but this teum shapes is jeust
the waant o starns. Thay glup

the orange lowe o the yotun
at colors aa Orcadia.
Thay glup her geyran face.

Noor sets the skiff tae drift
an leans back in her seat,
een clossed. The wracks sloom by.

"What are they?" speirs Darling,
an the arkaeolojist bairks
a laagh. "Exactly," says Noor.

Darling goes to see the wrecks

She thought there'd be something more, but these emptyhungry
shapes are just the wantneed of stars. They gulpcatchswallow

the orange flameglowflickerflare of the gas giant that colours all of
Orcadia. They gulpcatchswallow her covetously staring face.

Noor sets the skiff to drift and leans back in her seat, eyes closed.
The wrecks slideslinkdream by.

"What are they?" asks Darling, and the archaeologist barkcoughwarns
a laugh. "Exactly," says Noor.

"Exactly." Darling is grabbid.
"But surely—I mean—they must—"
"Look," says Noor, no appenan

her een. "There's no known substance
which can form constructions
this vast or regular, and no

sign of a life that made them.
So." An Darling turns
awey. "I'm sorry," sheu says.

    "Exactly." Darling is vexed. "But surely—I mean—they must—" "Look,"
says Noor, not opening
    her eyes. "There is no known substance which can form constructions
this vast or regular, and no
    sign of a life that made them. So." And Darling turns away. "I'm sorry,"
she says.

Olaf Lighter hishan his bairn tae sleep

The sang is aald an the week by
wis the bairn cheust takkan twatree steps:
a hairdly-human knitch o need,
but waakan. The bairn's een is clossan
an unner the sang is Olaf's quaistions:

Will thay tak tae the Wheel's ducts,
smoo roon labs o a night, clim
as possessed o a tail, dore tae be taen
oot i'the yoles, lairn the hidden
neuks o the staetion an naems o the Lights?

Olaf the Lighter lulling his child to sleep

The song is old and last week the child just took a few steps: a hardly-human bundletruss of need, but walking. The child's eyes are closing, and under the song are Olaf's questions:

Will they enjoyexplore the Wheel's ducts, hidesneak into food laboratories at night, climb as though they had a tail, demandpesterbabble to be taken out in the boats, learn the hidden nooks of the station and names of Lights?

36

Like him, his mither an hers, langsyne,
pure mixter-maxter staetion fock,
makkan a piece taegither, sharan
the bit thir gotten, no kennan grund?
Or will this bairn be somtheen new?

Ten year an thay'll be gittan as taall
as thir room is wide, an lairnan grand
astrometry an polietics.
The polietics thir gotten here
is cheust enogh tae dael thir maet

an finiesh a teullyo ithoot a body
murdert. Thir ae planet tae meisur.
The only subjeck Olaf enjoyed
at the skeul wis histry. He kens the warld
is noo expandan faaster again,

    Like Olaf, his mother, and hers, a long way back, a very diverse mix
of station people, making a placedistancepartwhile together, sharing the
littlepiece they have and not knowing groundplanets. Or will this child be
something new?
    Ten years and they will be growing as tall as the room is wide, and
learning goodbig astrometry and politics. The politics they have here is
just enough to sharedividefate their foodmeat
    and finish a fightbroilstruggle without anyone being murdered. There's
one planet to measure. The only subject Olaf enjoyed at school was history.
He knows that the world is now expanding faster again,

an that new speeds tak newer warlds,
channels tae sype Orcadia whill aa
that bides is histry, staetion gaen
tae bruckalaetion, voyd hulks.
So mibbe this bairn'll waant tae brak

the next speed barrier, or the next?
In this peedie bunk, draeman
o cities, draeman o meanan more.
Or draeman a love fer a dwynan piece?
Whit wan o this futurs is bruckit mosst?

    and that new speeds bring newer worlds, channels to draindry Orcadia
until all that waitstaylives is history: station gone to ruindestruction,
emptyabandoned hulks. So maybe this child will want to break
    the next speed barrier, or the next? In this little bedbunk, dreaming
of cities, dreaming of meaning more? Or dreaming a love for a
pinefadewithering placedistancepartwhile? And which of these futures is
the most brokenrubbishruined?

Gunnie Margitsbairn nyargs at thir mither

"Ach mither!" thay say. "Thoo kens A'm waantan
tae sail wi thee! Whit wey will thoo
no tell the Ting tae pit me on
thee yole?" The week's Ting is meant

tae gyde the staetion's folk atween
wirk thir waantan an wirk at's needed,
but Gunnie's petitioned tae tak tae the Lights
fer a puckle o year an nivver been.

Thir mither stirs the protein soup
an says feenty-thing. "Mither!"
Gunnie's voyce is clangan aff
the thin waas o the quaaters thay share.

Gunnie, Margit's child, naggrumblefaulttaunts their mother

  "Ach, mother!" they say. "You know I wantneed to sail with you!
Whathowwherewhy won't you tell the Council to assign me to your boat?"
The weekly Council is meant
  to manageguidecontrol the station's people between work they want
and work that's needed, but Gunnie's petitioned to work gathering Lights
for several years and never been.
  Their mother stirs the protein soup and says nothing. "Mother!"
Gunnie's voice is clanging off the thin walls of the quarters they share.

An Margit turns. "I waant gets notheen,"
sheu says like spittan feeskid maet.
"An the Lights gets notheen an aa. Hid's me
at's keepid thoo fae the bleudy yoles."

Gunnie's skrek isno oot
thir thrapple whan Margit lifts the speun.
"Stoop! Dinno thoo come tae me
wi thee waant." Margit ladles soup,

ignoran Gunnie's hawie glower.
Sheu scraeps the pot an disno waste
a thowt. As Gunnie brattles oot,
thir mither taks thir bowl an aets.

And Margit turns. "I wantneed gets nothing," she says like spitting putridmouldy foodmeat. "And the Lights gets nothing either. It's me that's kept you off the bloody boats."

Gunnie's yellscreech hasn't left their throat when Margit lifts the spoon. "Quiet! Don't come to me with your wantneed." Margit ladles soup,

ignoring Gunnie's palewan scowlstare. She scrapes the pot and doesn't waste a thoughtmorsel. As Gunnie crashrushstorms out, their mother takes their bowl and eats.

Øyvind Grower an Eynar o the Hoose tak a eveneen class

Thay wir bairns at the skeul taegither,
an noo hid's tretty year gaen,
an thir listenan tae this bairn

fae the bairn toons o Tau Ceti
wi a croose reid face
lairn a class o adults

reputaetional capietal,
brandeen niches, rare
haaf aathenticity . . .

Eynar taks notts noo,
as geud as Øyvind's fae skeul.
Thay canno leuk at each ither.

Øyvind the Grower and Eynar the Landlord take an evening class

They went to school together as children, and now it's thirty years later and they're listening to this child

from the child towncities of Tau Ceti with a smugmerrypleased face learnteach a class of adults

reputational capital, branding niches, rareunusual deep space authenticity . . .

Eynar takes notes now, as good as Øyvind's were at school. They can't look at each other.

Eftir, whan that Brenna,
maed up like a Martian,
tries tae tise thaim tae

her teum raedeen grup –
"Revolutionary Thowt
in Pre-Stellar Eart,"

says sheu, keen as tae cut –
thir gled o the antic distraction
(tho thay jentle refuse the lass),

fer than this twa taal men
dinno hiv tae blether
aboot the peedie chairs,

or age, or wirk, or Light,
or whit lot o credits
this haep o dirt is warth.

Afterwards, when that Brenna, adornedhappyinvented like a Martian, tries to coaxcajole them to
her emptyhungry reading group – "Revolutionary Thought in Pre-Stellar Earth,"
says she, keen enough to cut – they're glad of the amusinggrotesque distraction (though they gently refuse the girlwoman),
because then these two tall men don't have to talkchatramble about the little chairs
or age, or work, or Light, or how manymuch credits this heap of mudshitrubbish is worth.

42

A alt-arkaeolojist visits wi Noor

"It's simple," he says, his wide blue een
bright, skrankie haands puskan.
"When you look at it right. They're not
wrecks. Not broken. They are—they are
a message we don't know how to decode."
Noor freesks an sibbles her tea, tuinan
her lugs tae the Varday module's meusic.
"Why else would they be here, in the path
of our expansion? Ready for us
to find? For us? Why else would the doors
have been left open?" The metal cruin:
solar plants, atmospheric
regulaetors, gravietaetional
spin. "And who, well, who else?
There's no one else, no contact, no trace—"

An alt-archaeologist pays a visit to Noor

"It's simple," he says, his wide blue eyes bright, his
scraggymeagrespidery hands fidgetfussgustsearching. "When you look
at it right. They're not wrecks. Not broken. They are—they are a message
we don't know how to decode." Noor smiles falsely and sipslurps her tea,
tuning her ears to the Varday module's music. "Why else would they be
here, in the path of our expansion? Ready for us to find? For us? Why else
would the doors have been left open?" The metal humtunesongwail: solar
plants, atmospheric regulators, gravitational spin. "And who, well, who
else? There's no one else, no contact, no trace—"

Whanivver sheu gaed tae a surface noo
sheu coudno sleep until sheu'd fiegured
whit wis missan an tirled the soond
o her pod tae *injine*. "—so it must be us!"
His face is pride an revelaetion.
"It's either us in the past or us
in the future. And really, you know, that's the same,
I mean—" Noor taks his tagsie slaets,
leuks trou his hoppless calculaetions,
trou her feet, trou the deck,
trou the plies o Varday's skin,
trou the quiet wracks haaden
in tow, tae the haaf an deeper yet.
Whit soonds sheu'd find oot thir, whit waves.

Whenever she went to a surface now she couldn't sleep until she'd
worked out what was missing and turntwistspinwhirled the sound of her
pod to *engine*. "—so it must be us!" His face is pride and revelation. "It's
either us in the past or us in the future. And really, you know, that's the
same, I mean—" She takes his shabbydisordered slates, looks through
his hopeless calculations, through her feet, through the floor, through the
strata of Varday's skin, through the quiet wrecks held in tow, to deep space
and deeper. What sounds she'd find out there, what waves.

Higgie the Codd clocks aff

Sheu snecks the monietors wan by wan,
fer the plant tae idle the sleepan oors.

Sheu lillilus tae her machines,
her aald face in ivry gless

– but no, yin's no her face. Sheu blenks.
A karl sportan some kinno helmet

(but maed o some kinno metal? an glessless?)
is skirlan – but silent. He chairges the screen.

A flist o Light. Sheu shuts her een
but feels the sair lowe trou her lids.

Higgie the Coder clocks off

She turns off the monitors one by one, for the plant to idle the
sleeping hours.

She lullabies to her machines, her old face in each grey mirrorglass
– but no, that's not her face. She blinks. An older man wearing a kind
of helmet

(but made of a kind of metal? and without glass?) is shrieksqualling –
but silent. He charges the screen.

A rushrageboastbang of Light. She shuts her eyes, but feels the
harshdireoppressive flameglowflickerflare through her lids.

45

But eftir a spell sheu peeks an than
thir notheen thir. Nae willan Light,

nae flegsome man. Sheu skites ootbye
an slams the doar, an waits ahint hid,

an sings a peedie bit looder, looder
as the hivvy clankan an crashan inbye

at isno the weel-kent tick o the plant
mairkan hids time, but soonds instaed—

no—ya—no—but—
like steel brakkan steel, a draem o a sword.

But after a short while she looks and then there's nothing there.
No wildwandering Light,
    no terrifying man. She slidebounceshoots outside and slams the door,
and waits behind it,
    and sings a little louder, louder than the heavy clanking and crashing
inside
    that is not the familiar tick of the plant marking time, but sounds
instead—
    no—yes—no—but—like steel breaking steel, a dream of a sword.

Astrid meets the visietor, Darling

Astrid's sketchan the yoles at a pierheid on Central,
cosh i'the neuk anunder a pilot light,
whan Darling, no lukkan, snappers atwart her, dingan
her styluses ower the skitey deck o the pier.
Thay waatch the gadjets hurl intae the clifts,
Darling speldered intae Astrid's skirt.

Darling's haep o sorries an offers o credit
is as gabsie as Astrid's reassurance is blate.
"I wirno uissan thaim. Better ithoot."
Darling trys tae mak the fykie transietion
fae shock tae blether wi "Are you visiting too?"
an gars somtheen a weys more precious gang.

Astrid meets the visitor, Darling

Astrid is sketching the boats at a pierhead on Central,
snugquiethappyintimate in the nook under a pilot light, when Darling,
not looking, stumblestammers across her, knocking her styluses over the
slippery deckfloor of the pier. They watch the gadgets speedthrowrolldrive
into the crackchinks, Darling spreadsplit over Astrid's lap.

Darling's many apologies and offers of credit are as voluble as
Astrid's reassurance is shydiffident. "I wasn't using them. Better without."
Darling tries to make the trickyfussyrestless transition from shock to
talkchatramble with "Are you visiting too?" and causeforces something
more precious to go.

But wi the offer o tea, Astrid gies
tae Darling whit sheu's waantan: lowses the vouels
in her spaekeen, nods an smiles whan Darling yatters
on aboot community, the community,
fills the visietor's lugs wi the new aaldness
o her staetion haem, spaeks whit sheu disno ken.

An eftir, eftir tea turns tae spirits,
kennan her ploys is waatched by ivry lighter
i'the Hoose, cheussan no tae mynd, seean
the meanan o the lunt in Darling's een,
carean that sheu disno care, sheu laaghs
at the dunt o the invitaetion an follows the wife.

But with the offer of tea, Astrid can perform for Darling what she
wants: loosens the vowels in her speech, nods and smiles as Darling
rambles about community, the community, fills the visitor's ears with the
new oldness of her station home, tells her what she doesn't know.

And later, after tea becomes spirits, knowing her actiondecisiongames
are watched by every lighter in the House, choosing not to
rememberknowreflectwill, seeing the meaning of the flamesparklight
in Darling's eyes, caring that she does not care, she laughs at the
shockchancestrike of the invitation and follows the woman.

Thir touchan's stimmerie joy, trivvlan, agglan,
airtan, error, hixan, delight. Thay both
ken the movs an maan unlairn them noo
fer this new body's waas, windows, doars.
Astrid taks a guff o Mars again,
an Darling, discovry. Thir tongs tak a gless.

Than eftir, whan the cruisies brighten tae morneen,
wi Darling yet sleepan, Astrid busks an leuks
fae porthole tae bunk, fae the tide tae Darling's hair,
an speirs o the gods, at dinno exist, if
thir both fund whit thay waant, or need, or no,
or if thir maed hid, or if hid ivver metters.

Their touch is stumblestammering joy, fumblefiddling,
messdirtconfusion, searchfinding, error, laughhiccuping, delight. They both
know the moves and must unlearn them now for this new personbody's
walls, windows, doors. Astrid tastes a stinkpuffsnortnonsense of Mars
again, and Darling, discovery. Their tongues drink.

Then later, when the lamps brighten to morning, with Darling still
asleep, Astrid dressprepares and looks from porthole to bedbunk, from the
seatimetide to Darling's hair, and asks of the gods, who do not exist, if they
have both found what they want, or need, or not, or if they have created it,
or if it ever matters.

Twa

Darling an Astrid waatch a Lightstoor

Darling is greetan. "I've never,"
sheu says, "I've never . . ." An Astrid
kens, but canno decide,
seean the stoor o Lights,
the whips, the reid rivan
an gowd glisks, the skyran
dancers ower the curve
o a roilan warld, the dillan,
the braeth, the lithy, the paece,
the dunt as the planet-braid
linkwark o Lights, taegither,
sweys in a stark straik
ower the lip o sight,
whither o no tae say,
"Aye, but I mynd whan I
wir peedie thay wir more."

Darling and Astrid watch a Lightstorm
    Darling is weeping. "I've never," she says, "I've never . . ." And Astrid
knows, but can't decide, seeing the stormstrifestrainspeeddust of
Lights, the gustdarttwistattacks, the red wrenchripbreaking and gold
glimpsegleampuffthrillscares, the gaudyshining dancers over the curve of
a roiling world, the dimfadedying, the breath, the lullgappath, the peace,
the shockchancestrike as the planet-wide linkwork of Lights, as one,
swerveswingsways in a thickviolent streak, over the edge of sight, whether
or not to say, "Yes, but I rememberknowreflectwill when I was little there
were more."

Inga raeds a airticle aboot the Lights

The swaeran taks Øyvind runnan
fae the kitcheen. "Bastards! Shite-fer-braens!
Fuck." He pits a jentle haand
on her back an hings ower the screen.

The airticle sheu's raedan's aboot
a submission tae the Federal Ting
on the theoretiecal basis an
structural possiebility o

extra-corporeal photon network
consciousness, an the push
fer furder study. The bigsy heidline's
white: CAN LIGHTS THINK?

Inga reads an article about the Lights
The swearing brings Øyvind running from the kitchen. "Bastards!
Shit-for-brains! Fuck!" He puts a gentle hand on her back and leanhangs
over the screen.

The article she's reading is about a submission to the Federal Council
on the theoretical basis and structural possibility of

extra-corporeal photon network consciousness, and the push for
further study. The bigproudconceited headline is white: CAN LIGHTS
THINK?

"Can thay fuck!" says Inga. "I dinno
fuckan care if thir fuckan conscious!
or fuckan dansan! or fuckan fuckan!
Fuck!" Tentie, Øyvind trists

her shudder. "I ken," he says, an sheu,
"Thir jeuce i'the drives an that's maet on the taeble
an hid's haird enogh tae land a daecent
haal o Light ithoot fuckan

studies an xenobiolojists
an airmchair philosophers
an Fermi fucks!" Inga's greetan
noo, an Øyvind's fingers bris

intae her dilderan airms in comfort.
"Alaen," sheu says. "Can thay no see
wir aye been alaen? Will aye be alaen?"
Øyvind can only reply, "I ken."

⚙

    "Can they fuck!" says Inga, and, "I don't fucking care if they're fucking
conscious! or fucking dancing! or fucking fucking! Fuck!" Øyvind,
carefulwatchful, squeezehugpressthirsts
    her shoulder. "I know," he says, and she, "There's juice in the drives
and that's foodmeat on the table and it's hard enough to land a decent
haulcatch of Light without fucking
    studies and xenobiologists and armchair philosophers and Fermi
fucks!" Inga's weeping now, and Øyvind's fingers squeezepressbruise
    her tremblingjerking arms in comfort. "Alone," she says. "Can't they
see we've always been alone? Will always be alone?" And Øyvind can only
reply, "I know."

Higgie the Codd seeks expert advice

"Thoo kens aboot this things," sheu says tae Noor,
    as the arkaeolojist gans at the wracks.

"Pardon?" says Noor, than, "No. I'm not a psychologist,"
    pittan Higgie's biss up. "Hid wisno me braens.

A'm no gyte. Hid wis somtheen ither,
    somtheen scientific, like thee ships."

"We don't know they're ships," says Noor, wishan
    sheu wis wi thaim noo, "and I don't see what

they have to do with dreams of ancient swordsmen."
    "Hid wisno a draem! If hid wis a draem,

Higgie the Coder seeks expert advice

"You know about these things," she says to Noor, as the archaeologist staregazeyawns out at the wrecks.

"Pardon?" says Noor, then, "No. I'm not a psychologist," raising Higgie's hackles. "It wasn't in my head.

I'm not crazy. It was something else, something scientific, like your ships."

"We don't know they're ships," says Noor, wishing she was with them now, "and I don't see what

they have to do with dreams of ancient swordsmen." "It wasn't a dream! If it was a dream,

whit wey is me doars hammered, me screens smashed?
He cam fae nopiece, an back tae nopiece he gaed

an I waant tae ken hoo." Noor shrugs. "I've been with you here
for over a year, and can't tell you anything real

about my own work, let alone armoured men
appearing from the ether. But," sheu adds,

sofnan, seean madram turn tae pickloo,
feelan hid fillan her crampit, caald offiece,

no waantan tae aye be awey oot the edge o the Wheel,
"You've mynded me on about reports of not

unrelated incidents on other
inner stations. Distance, isolation,

whathowwherewhy are my doors hammered, my screens all smashed?
He came from nowhere, and he went back to nowhere
and I want to know how." Noor shrugs. "I've been with you here for
over a year, and can't tell you anything real
about my own work, let alone armoured men appearing from the ether.
But," she adds,
softening, seeing ragetroublegrief turn to panic, feeling it filling her
cramped, cold office,
not wanting to always be away out on the edge of the Wheel, "You've
reminded me about reports of not
unrelated incidents on other inner stations. Distance, isolation,

collective realities, et cetera.
      I've got some papers here." "A'm tellan thee,"

says Higgie, thight, "hid isno a braen thing.
      Hid's a time thing. Thoo keep thee paepers,

an tell me whar tae raed aboot time." Sheu's siccar
      wi a dizzen decades o haadan an spaekan her mind.

So Noor swipes ower the naems o enogh paepers
      in speculative temporal mechanics

tae keep the injineer occupyd,
      tae keep her, Noor lippens, fae coman back fer weeks,

an burns a few o thaim tae her awn slaet
      tae ameuse hersel whan sheu's notheen tae deu.

collective realities, et cetera. I have some papers here." "I'm telling you,"
says Higgie, tight-lipped, "it's not a brain thing. It's a time thing. Keep
your papers,
      and tell me where to read about time." Higgie's stableseveresteadfast
from a dozen decades of holding and speaking her mind.
      So Noor swipes over the names of enough papers in speculative
temporal mechanics
      to keep the engineer occupied, to keep her, Noor expects, from coming
back for weeks,
      and downloads a few of them to her own slate to amuse herself when
she has nothing to do.

Eynar snecks up

The widden worm sails trou the Hoose's waas.
No wi a skirpan o steel an a sprettan o ruives,
but trou, like a laser wi flesh, a neutrino wi
a planet, a ganfer wi a iron doar.

Eynar wis stackan chairs an moppan the deck.
The baest cam fae ahint. Hearan a knark,
he golders, "Clossed!" an turns an sees the mulls
shaan the teeth. The worm is broon an shinan,

an on hids back twa dizzen rootan fock.
Hids face is frozen. Hids reid weengs dunder.
An Light maks reefu plays alang hids lent,
hids shields an graith an reeg an fock alowe.

Eynar closes up
    The wooden snakedragonworm sails through the walls of the House.
Not with a ripsqueaktearing of steel and a startstripburstjumping of rivets,
but through, like a laser with flesh, a neutrino with a planet, an omenghost
with an iron door.
    Eynar was stacking chairs and mopping the floor. The animalmonster
came from behind. Hearing a creakcrackcrunch, he yelllaughroars, "Closed!"
and turns and sees the lips baring the teeth. The snakedragonworm is
brown and shining,
    and on its back are two dozen roarbellowing people. Its face is frozen.
Its red wings rumblebeatthunder. And Light makes madfuriousfrenzied
plays along its length, its shields and gear and rigging and people
flameglowflickerflaring.

59

Eynar skreks. The sealess ship flees trou
the next waa, no laevan a sign the Hoose
an hids man is willan at haem: notheen unless
a cuppid bucket an a reek o saalt.

Eynar screeches. The sealess ship flies through the next wall, leaving
no sign the House and its man are lostwildwandering at home: nothing
except an overturned bucket and a stinksmoke of salt.

Darling an Astrid tak a waak trou the wynds o Meginwick

The wynds is lit by cruisies set
tae Stannart Days, peedie suns

i'the girders lightan thir steps. Thay waak
the nerrow weys o Astrid's myndeen.

Roon this cunyo, the skeul; roon this,
the bruck byres, whar Astrid's blide

tae spy young fock is gloweran yet;
furder, the bell thay'd gang tae in pairs;

here, the Haa whar the wynds meet,
whar the Ting sets fees an lots thir quaaters,

Darling and Astrid take a walk through the corridors of Meginwick
The corridors are lit by lamps set to Standard Days, little suns
in the girders lighting their steps. They walk the narrow ways of
Astrid's giftremembrancememory.
Round this cornernook, the school; round this, the rubbishscrap barns,
where Astrid is happyfondpleased
to seespot young people still scowlstaring; further, the bubblebell
they'd go to in pairs;
here, the Hall where the corridors meet, where the Council sets
wagesprices and drawallocates quarters,

whar benks is shuitten back fer dansan.
Darling trys tae listen, but

hid's that peedie, an bye the waas
is the tide, the starns, an aalwarld things.

Thir haands sweeng closs, touch, twine,
pull back, touch more. An than: "Astrid?"

Thay birl, touchan yet, but Astrid
steps awey an the uncan body

says, "Hid's nivver thee?" The body
is Gunnie, at twal year ago wis Astrid's

inseparable freend, at ten year ago
gat nyargie, an thir no spocken ava

    where benchshelves are shoved back for dances. Darling tries to listen,
but
    it's so little, and just through these walls is the seatimetide, the stars,
and things from an older world.
    Their hands swing close, touch, entwine, pull back, touch more. And
then: "Astrid?"
    They whirlrushdancespin, still touching, but Astrid steps away and the
strangerweird personbody
    says, "That's never you?" The personbody is Gunnie, who twelve years
ago was Astrid's
    inseparable friend, who ten years ago got tiregrumbleboring, and they
haven't spoken at all

fae Astrid teuk the langship tae Mars.
"An wha's this?" speirs Gunnie, smirkan.

Thay wir snatchets o bairns, but Gunnie
is wallie nou wi shairp dairk een

an Astrid's forgotten hoo tae deu this.
Sheu swanders trou speiran at Gunnie's faimly,

giean her news, myndan on only
tae share the things sheu's fine wi aa

the fock aa ower the staetion hearan
in twatree oor, or mibbe less.

Darling waatches the clashan pair,
no unnerstannan enogh tae spaek,

since Astrid took the longship to Mars. "And who's this?" asks Gunnie,
smiling.
They were punyworthlessrascally children, but Gunnie now is
bighealthybeautiful with sharp dark eyes,
and Astrid has forgotten how to do this. She stumblewanders through
asking after Gunnie's family,
giving her news, rememberknowreflectwilling only to share the things
she doesn't mind
the people all over the station hearing within a few hours, maybe less.
Darling watches the noisygossiping pair, not understanding enough to
speak,

smilan but feelan a ropp hank aff
as sheu faas backleens intae space.

An Astrid's soondan appen, but keeps
her innerly nirts gairded. Sheu smiles,

promieses thay'll spaek, cheerios,
an firm taks Darling's bombazed haand.

    smiling but feeling a rope uncoil as she falls backwards into space.
    And Astrid sounds open, but keeps her
inmostshelteredintimateaffectionate crumbknots guarded. She smiles,
    promises they'll speak, says goodbye, and firmly takes Darling's
bewilderstupified hand.

Thay spaek aboot Mars

"So wha's thee fock?" speirs Astrid, but
Darling's reply is, "Boring! You don't
want to know." "Thoo kens mine!" says Astrid,
but things wi thaim is ower caller
fer her tae be a needle or
a hammer. "Whar'd ye bide, than?"

Darling describes the muckle domms
an tooers o Chryse, weel enogh
tae be convinceen, aboothaans
wi true. Astrid kieks a eebroo,
fer Chryse wis ower gowd an gated
fer Astrid's toosie college crood.

They speak about Mars

"So, tell me about your family," asks Astrid, but Darling's reply is,
"Boring! You don't want to know." "You know about mine!" says Astrid,
but things between them are too freshcleanhealthy for her to be a needle
or a hammer. "Where did you waitstaylive, then?"

Darling describes the greatbig domes and towers of Chryse,
well enough to be convincing, close to the truth. Astrid kicks an
eyebrow, because Chryse was far too wealthy and gated for Astrid's
roughshaggyrowdy college crowd.

"A'm only seen hid fae apae Ascraeus.
Hid's a peedie bit peedier fae thir."
Darling snushes. "Too peedie for me.
This is more my size." Sheu spraeds
her airms, raxan oot the tap
o the mintie taing o the mintie staetion,

tae haad twa meuns an a normous o starns.
"I miss it," says Astrid, an Darling's ferly
paalled. "Hid's true. No jeust me freends,
but bidan somepiece I coud be . . ."
"Be what?" "Be onybody. Or no
mesel. Or jeust no hiv tae be.

  "I've only seen it from up on Ascraeus. It's a lot littler from there."
Darling snorts. "Too little for me. This is more my size." She spreads her
arms, stretchreachexpanding out of the top of the tiny promontory of the
tiny station,
  to hold two moons and a huge number of stars. "I miss it," says Astrid,
and Darling's veryfairly astonishthwarted. "It's true. Not just my friends,
but waitstayliving somewhere I could be . . ." "Be what?" "Be anybody.
Or not myself. Or just not have to be.

Oot thir, wi that pile o fock, that gret
a lot tae deu, thoo disno hiv
tae be." Darling haads her haand.
"But you still liked to climb the highest
mountains in the solar system?"
"Yass. Else hid wis gey haird tae see."

Out there, with too many people, so much to do, you don't have to be."
Darling holds her hand. "But you still liked to climb the highest mountains
in the solar system?" "Yes. Otherwise it was pretty hard to see."

Inga an Olaf spaek bisness

"Whit like, beuy?" sheu says.
Sheu kens fine weel whit like.
Olaf is by fer his tea,
an sits ithoot drinkan or spaekan.

Sheu taks a haad o the wheel.
"Thoo're thinkan A'm wirkan the bott
an the crew ower haird." He sprets.
"Hid isno jeust aboot me!

Fer A'm gotten me bairn,
an hid's jeust me thir gotten,
an Erlend is haen his third,
an Erika's parent's no weel,

Inga and Olaf talk business

"What's going on, friendmanboy?" she says. She knows perfectly well
what's going on. Olaf has come to her for tea, and sits without drinking or
speaking.

She takes charge. "You think I'm working the ship and the crew too
hard." He startstripburstjumps. "It's not just me!

Because I have my baby, and they've only got me, and Erlend has had
his third, and Erika's parent is sick,

an Ingrid—" "Deus thoo no think
A'm kennan that? We canno—"
"We canno gang oot ivry day!"
Olaf is ferly gowlan.

"We can an we maan," says Inga,
"or whit'll thee bairn aet,
or Erlend's, or Erika's parent?
Is hid no creches an nurses

whan wiss wi bairns maan wirk?"
"Is hid no common stores
whan thee credits is thin?"
he snashes, an Inga gets quiet

an sad. "Hid isno me,"
sheu says. "Hid's Orcadia.
The Ting kens whit's coman.
If thoo an me tak noo,

and Ingrid—" "Don't you think I know? We can't—" "We can't go out
every day!" Olaf is really bellowcrying.

"We can and we must," Inga says, "or what will your babychild eat,
or Erlend's, or Erika's parent? Aren't there creches and nurses

when those of us with children have to work?" "Aren't there common
stores when you're short on credits?" he snapbites, and Inga grows quiet

and sad. "It's not me," she says. "It's Orcadia. The Council knows what's
coming. If you and I take now,

69

thir'll be notheen next year,
or eftir, whan the Lights
is anteran, an the shippeen,
an aa wir needan tae bide.

Wir wirkan while we can."
Quiet, but haird. Olaf's
tea is caald. "Hid isno
that bad," he says, but hid is.

   there will be nothing next year, or later, when the Lights are
rareunusual, and the shipping, and everything we need to waitstaylive.
   We're working while we can." Quiet, but hard. Olaf's tea is cold.
"It's not that bad," he says, but it is.

Astrid casts back tae a pal fae the college

The cast sheu gits by slow packet is pangit
wi sarcasm. Whit like is sheu noo i'the inner
wylds? Is sheu been reprogrammed yet
by the spacers? Deus sheu mynd whit like is the taste
o a gress-fed staek? Whit like is the yird o Mars?

Whit like is the smell o caller air? The bizz
o her jack pluggid in tae civiliesaetion?
Hoo tae dance? The election, the sit-in, the mairch?
Her social credits is plumman the reid; jeust whit
deus sheu think sheu's deuan? Whan wad sheu come haem?

Astrid casts back to a friend from art school

The message she receives by slow packet is fullbursting with sarcasm. How is she doing now in the inner wilds? Has she been reprogrammed yet by the spacers? Does she rememberknowreflectwill how a grass-fed steak tastes? How Mars' groundworldsoil feels?

How freshcleanhealthy air smells? The buzzbustle of her jack plugged in to civilisation? How to dance? The election, the sit-in, the march? Her social credits are plumbing the red; just what does she think she is doing? When would she come home?

Astrid gans intae the lens o her caster
an sends afyoag o a laagh tae the funs, hersel,
her haem, an yaps aboot the tarf an retro
chairm o astro-industrial arkietecture
an hoo the yotun's yallo swaalls her braeth.

Sheu smiles an lees aboot the space o space,
an hoo sheu's deuan that grand a wark oot here.
(Her slaet bides teum yet; the vacuums atween
the biggeens o Deep Wheel Orcadia fill
o traffic, industry, mynd, wirds and waith.)

An than sheu says, "Listen," an records the deep
mum o Aikeray's injines, the bed an baet
o aa her life. An than sheu says, "Thoo
shoud come," if only tae insense hersel
thir onytheen here that sheu coud ivver share.

    Astrid staregazeyawns into the lens of her caster and sends a big
laugh at the jokegames, herself, her home, and talknagbarks about the
harshbitter and retro charm of astro-industrial architecture, and how
the gas giant's yellow swellwaves her breath.
    She smiles and lies about the space of space, and how she does so
much work out here. (Her slate waitstaylives emptyhungry still; the
vacuums between the structures of Deep Wheel Orcadia are full of traffic,
industry, memorythoughtmeaning, words and flotsamstrays.)
    And then she says, "Listen," and records the deep
hummumblewhisperword of Aikeray's engines, the bed and rhythm of all
her life. And then she says, "You should come," if only to convinceimpress
herself that there's anything here that she could ever share.

Darling jacks the news

Sheu wun tae twa day afore lukkan. Days o paece,
forgettan, pretendan sheu wisno traikid by histry
(or faimly, whit's aye the sam thing). An paece is grand,
but the coorse yeuk tae ken if paece is true
or no, an if hid's gaan tae end, returns.
Sheu digs intae her pack fer the vacuum gansey,
unhaps her bauchelt pod an jacks hid in.

This weys in the data transfer's driltan –
enerjy's dear fer aa thay mak hid here –
an whan the infodump is deun hid's like
a patchwark: twa-month-aald reports comed oot
by slow packets, hilligo advertiseens
an feenty news by faast packets, an only
urjent bulletins by ansible.

Darling plugs into the news

She reachtravelachieved two days before looking. Days of peace,
forgetting, pretending she wasn't trudgetrackexhausted by history (or
family, which is always the same thing). And peace is goodbig, but the
roughhardnasty itch to know if peace is true or not, and if it's going
to end, returns. She digs into her pack for the vacuum sweaterjersey,
unwrapcoverbundles her wornroughdiscarded pod and plugs it in.

This far in the data transfer is slowdreamdawdling – energy's
expensive even though they make it here – and when the infodump
is done it's like a patchwork: two-month-old reports delivered by slow
packets, flightygiddynoisycrazy adverts and cursednothing news by fast
packets, and only urgent bulletins by ansible.

The loup tae haaf is ferfil gien the lie
tae infienit informaetion alwis on,
an hid's waant. An noo sheu disno care whit's on
on Mars, ivry teullyo maed wanwirt
by space an time. The rampan wirds atween
the ooter Nordren Fed an Angle colonies
is that closs tae claikan sheu jeust ignores thaim.

Sheu ransels instaed fer her aald naem an face.
Whan thir notheen new – jeust the sam
thraets an offers tae thieves an arbitraetors,
ithoot a witter o roon whit wan o the starns
sheu's birlan noo – sheu shills her peedie pod,
happan hids cell in a sark, hids screen in anither.
Hid isno paece, but hid's somtheen closs.

The jumpspringvault to deep space has veryfearfully given the lie to
infinite information always on, and its wantneed. And now she doesn't
care what's happening on Mars, every fightbroilstruggle made worthless
by space and time. The simmersputtermuddlefussing words between outer
Northern Federation and Angle colonies are so close to gossipclucking she
just ignores them.

She searchsnoopransacks instead for her old name and face. When
there's nothing new – just the same threats and threatoffers to thieves
and arbitrators, without any signguideknowingfishhook of round which
of the stars she's whirlrushdancespinning now – she husks her little pod,
wrapcoverbundling its power source in a shirt and its screen in another.
It's not peace, but it's something close.

Noor needs a drink

"Yir no come by ower affens," says Eynar, awey.
Noor sits hersel alaen at the bar. "My loss,"
sheu says. "I thought I should get to know folk better."
"Thir no ower much tae ken." Noor flenches an poors

her uncan discomfort intae her soor drink.
Eynar sees an relents. "Whit like's yir wracks?"
"Big," sheu says. "Blank," sheu says. "Empty." An flenches again
at hoo sheu's lairned hid's ferfil grand tae be soor.

Abasht, sheu blethers on, sayan hoo
hid's gey bonnie here, hoo sheu loves it,
the coothie fock, and Eynar listens, ootward,
noddan. "No bad, ya, hid isno bad."

Noor needs a drink

"You haven't visited much," says Eynar, awaydeaddistracted. Noor sits
by herself at the bar. "My loss," she says. "I thought I should get to know
folk better." "There's not too much to know." Noor shiftflinches and pours

her strangerweird discomfort into her sourbitterrudemiserable drink.
Eynar sees and relents. "How are your wrecks?" "Big," she says. "Blank,"
she says. "Empty." And shiftflinches again at how she's learned that it's
veryfearfully goodbig to be sourbitterrudemiserable.

Abashed, she talkchatrambles on, saying how it's pretty finepretty here,
how she loves it, the friendlycomfortablepleasantunthreatening folk, and
Eynar listens, outwardreserveddistant, nodding. "Not bad, yes, it's not bad."

Noor disno see the barman's worm-taen widdrim
so sheu asks if Eynar is thowt o flittan,
ivver waanted tae bide somepiece ither.
The quaistion skites aff his slite an cuttit wirds.

"Hid'll deu." "We deu fine." "No bad."
Thir quiet a piece. He poors, sheu drinks, thay smile.
An a thowt comes tae Eynar at waarms him, o somtheen
he coud share wi this bonnie aakward body.

"If thoo waants tae ken fock better, come
tae the Dance Firstday next. Hid's wiss at wir best."
Noor coudno, sheu didno, sheu wadno waant tae impose,
disno think sheu'd be walcome, canno dance,

    Noor doesn't see the barman's worm-brought nightmaredazeconfusion,
so she asks if Eynar ever thought of leaveflyescaping, ever wanted to
waitstaylive somewhere else. The question slidebounceshoots off his
smoothstilllevel and cutcurt words.
    "It'll do." "We do well enough." "Not bad." They are quiet for a
placedistancepartwhile. He pours, she drinks, they smile. And a thought
comes to Eynar that warms him, of something he could share with this
finepretty awkward personbody.
    "If you want to know us folk better, come to the Dance next Firstday.
It's us at our best." Noor couldn't, she didn't, she wouldn't want to impose,
doesn't think she'd be welcome, can't dance,

but Eynar's insistan wi more an more blide wirds
as ony gien the night. Forbye, Noor waants
tae gang, an dance. Whan sheu's finished her drink,
he asks, "A'll see thee thir?" an Noor says, "Yass."

but Eynar's insisting with more and more happyfondpleased words
than any he's offered all night. Besides, Noor wants to go, and dance. When
she's finished her drink, he asks, "I'll see you there?" and Noor says, "Yes."

Øyvind's notions

Whan he's alaen,
the young eens gaen
or no assigned,

he taks a key
tae a private store
at's pangit wi maet.

The day, he curses:
The maet's green.
Øyvind sceups

the protein ashets
intae the chemiecal
reclamaetor,

Øyvind's ideaexperimentinventions
When he's alone, the young ones gone or not assigned,
he takes a key to a private store that's fullbursting with foodmeat.
Today, he curses: the foodmeat is green. Øyvind scoops
the protein serving dishes into the chemical reclamator,

pernickety, dights
wi sterile pads
tae stairt again.

The maet smoothy's
against the chance
o contamienaetion

or ony gokkan
o his notions.
Orcadia's maet

is weel-trusted:
why pret wi that?
The future's coman.

He's gotten somtheen
new – whan
the mix is right.

precisefussy, cleanwipes with sterile pads to start again.
The foodmeat hidey-hole is against the chancerisk of contamination
or any mockjokepranking at his ideaexperimentinventions.
Orcadia's maet
is well-trusted: why tamperplay with that? The future's coming.
He has something new – when the mix is right.

He disno think
tae chaenge the warld,
jeust waants tae plaese

his awn tongue.
He sets tae blendan
anither batch.

He doesn't think about changing the world, just wantneeds to please
his own tongue. He starts to blend another batch.

Astrid lairns Darling a new dance

Astrid kent this steps afore sheu coud spaek
(sheu wis a backerly spaeker): her mither held her
in fierdy airms an birled her roon an roon
the center o the Haa wi couples hurlan by.

Noo Astrid's haadan Darling wi siclike a grip
an coonts the dance's steps as meusic fills
the teum Ting Haa. Thir gotten a len
o twatree oor tae mak the visietor raedy.

Darling's laaghan. This dances is stootly ither
as whit she kens fae Mars. Thir no the perjink,
jenteel traed, traety an espionage
o her faithers' Chryse corporate functions. Thir no

Astrid teaches Darling a new dance
    Astrid knew these steps before she could speak (she was a
lateslow speaker: her mother held her in strongbriskworthy arms and
whirlrushspindanced her round and round the centre of the Hall, couples
speedthrowrolldriving by.
    Now Astrid holds Darling with the same grip and counts the dance's
steps as music fills the emptyhungry Council Hall. They've borrowed a few
hours to make the visitor ready.
    Darling's laughing. These dances are verystoutly different from what
she knows from Mars. They're not the primprecise and genteel trade,
treaties and espionage of her fathers' Chryse corporate functions, nor

the sensory-seutid low-gravity raves
apae Olympus Mons, cuithins will-willan
wi meusic in thir helmets, naeraboots
unteddert fae the reid an hirsty grund.

Sheu's lairnan noo tae mov her feet faaster,
wi aese an virr, an catchan noo the guff
o Astrid's sweit, an her awn. *Turn*, sheu thinks,
one-and-two-and-clap. "That's hid. No bad."

the sensory-suited low-gravity raves up on Olympus Mons,
immaturecoalfishrascals mind-wandering to the music in their helmets,
nearly untethered from the red and drybarrenstony ground.

Now she's learning to move her feet faster, with ease and vigourwhirr,
and now she's smellcatching the stinkpuffsnortnonsense of Astrid's sweat
and her own. *Turn*, she thinks, *one-and-two-and-clap.* "That's it. Not bad."

Astrid taks Darling haem fer dinner

"This is me new freend" – an the layers in "freend"
isno ferly clear an'll no be explaened.

Darling is winsome noo; sheu's somtheen ither
as the skarr thing o a toorist Astrid met.

A smile in her fernteckled face, rorie claes.
I'the mids o this faimly hid's like her body is lowan.

Mibbe the thowt o parents luntit performance.
Wi Darling's silence aboot her awn faithers,

Astrid's ower thankful fer Inga an Øyvind's
maet an kindness – until fair intae the meal

Astrid takes Darling home for dinner
    "This is my new friend" – and the layers in "friend" really aren't clear
and won't be explained.
    Darling is charmingattractive now: she's something other than the
frightenednervous tourist Astrid met.
    A smile in her freckled face, brightloud clothes. Among this family it's
like her personbody is flameglowflickerflaring.
    Maybe the thought of parents flamelightsparked performance. With
Darling's silence about her own fathers,
    Astrid's very grateful for Inga and Øyvind's foodmeat and kindness –
until well into the meal

sheu hears thir vooels roondan, thir consonants clippan,
thir wirds sweetchan tae marry Darling's awn,

an gits unspaekable barman. An whan her awn
"een" is "one" sheu sits quiet, waantan

a body tae notiece, her mither tae smile an say "Buddo"
an tak her back tae the aald faimly taeble,

but the hairt o Astrid's silence haes aafil gravity,
an so the conversaetion is faggan, faan,

is hearan hidsel, is less an less real gittan,
til hid's jeust Darling at's smilan an spaekan yet.

she hears their vowels rounding, their consonants clipping, their words
switching to matchequalmate Darling's own,
    and becomes unspeakably ragefrothseething. And when her own "een"
is "one" she goes quiet, wantneeding
    someone to notice, her mother to smile and say "FriendChildLove" and
with it bring her back to the old family table,
    but the heart of Astrid's silence has awful gravity, and so the
conversation driftfailflags, falls,
    hears itself, grows less and less real, till it's only Darling who's still
smiling and speaking.

Young Brenna at the Ting

Brenna's speechifyan. Sheu chants aboot the inherent
inequalities o the interstellar economy,
whit wey the extractive industrial laebor relaetions
in Light production noo require a radiecal
reimagienation o Orcadia's pouer,
whit wey the FtL drive wisno a thraet, but
a opportunity tae shaa the galaxy
whit wey tae wirk a better wey. Sheu spaeks gey weel.
Sheu wis been practiesan her argiements fer weeks.

Brenna at the Council

   Brenna's making a speech. She speaks affectedly about the inherent
inequalities of the interstellar economy, whathowwherewhy the extractive
industrial labour relations in Light production now require a radical
reimagination of Orcadia's power, about whathowwherewhy the Faster-
than-Light drive wasn't a threat but an opportunity to showpass the galaxy
whathowwherewhy to work a better way. She speaks pretty well. She has
been practising her arguments for weeks.

"Lass, thanks fer that," says Unn, the aaldest thir,
an aye the Chair thay dinno hiv. "Noo, the stores—"
"Haad on!" Brenna golders, horrid reid gittan.
"Ir we no gaan tae discuss whit A'm spaekan aboot?" "Yass, yass,"
says Unn, coothie an blide. "Wha's gotten somtheen thir waantan
or needan tae say cheust noo tae Brenna's clivver notions?"
The fill Haa is dainty silent. An silent yet.
Brenna didno ken tae practiese fer this, an Unn
is practiesed aa thir life. Unn hoasts. "Noo, the stores . . ."

    "Girlwoman, thanks for that," says Unn, the oldest there and
always the Chair they don't have. "Now, the stores—" "Hold on!"
Brenna yelllaughroars, growing veryhorribly red already. "Aren't
we going to discuss what I'm talking about?" "Yes, yes," says Unn,
friendlycomfortablepleasantunthreatening and happyfondpleased. "Who
has something they wantneed to say now to Brenna's very quickintelligent
ideaexperimentinventions?" The wholefull Hall is verydaintily silent. And
stays silent. Brenna didn't know to practise for this, and Unn has practised
all their life. Unn coughharrumphclears. "Now, the stores . . ."

Noor an Eynar spaek eftir the Ting

"I sayed tae see wiss at wir best,
no this," he says. Noor wis waatched
the meeteen, takkan notts. Sheu laaghs.
"It's better than a research committee."

Eynar's heid is tiftan fae ringan
an rallyan debate. "A'd tak a vott
instaed o this some days," he says,
an shrugs. Thay taak a waak i'the wynds.

"I wouldn't," says Noor. "At least you try
to build consensus, make things fair."
"Oh yass," says Eynar, an Noor kens noo
this ferly disno mean agreement.

Noor and Eynar speak after the Council

"I said to see us at our best, not this," he says. Noor had watched the
meeting, taking notes. She laughs. "It's better than a research committee."

Eynar's head is throbfestering from ringcirclebanging,
crowdquarrellurching debate. "I'd take a vote instead of this sometimes,"
he says, and shrugs. They go for a walk in the corridors.

"I wouldn't," says Noor. "At least you try to build consensus, make
things fair. "Oh yes," says Eynar, and Noor knows now this definitely
doesn't mean agreement.

"I doot thir no a system coud copp
wi whit this days is takkan wiss."
The Ting wis biggid fer manajan stocks,
resolvan contracks. Hids bleudiest wark

wis exile, no the ruinaetion
o tekno-economic chaenge.
"Is that why you didn't speak?" asks Noor.
"A'll spaek whan A'm gotten somtheen tae offer,"

he says, "an that'll no be till A'm—eh . . ."
He steps an leuks awey. "Until . . . ?"
"Ach, na. We're here." Thir by the Hoose.
Noor feels sheu's missan somtheen important

but feels that ivry day. The big man
leuks as lost as her. "Thoo're no
pit aff?" Sheu shaks her heid an smiles.
The invitaetion is somtheen new.

"I expect there isn't any system that could cope with what these
days hold for us." The Council was built for managing stocks, resolving
contracts. Its hardestbloodiest worktask
was exile, not the ruination of techno-economic change. "Is that why
you didn't speak?" asks Noor. "I'll speak when I have something to offer,"
he says, "And that won't be until I am—um . . ." He stops and looks
away. "Until . . . ?" "Ach, no. We're here." They're by the House. Noor feels
like she's missed something important,
but feels like that every day. The big man looks as lost as her. "You're
not put off?" She shakes her head and smiles. The invitation is something
new.

"But you'll have to teach me the steps," sheu says,
an waves a cheerio. Thir fock
waitan fer Eynar tae tak the drinks
fer the unofficial second meeteen.

Ivry ee is on the pair.
"Ach, wheesht," says Eynar, ahint the bar.
The goldereen's aither a anchor or
a hurlan wind. He taks the drinks.

"But you'll have to teach me the steps," she says, and waves goodbye.
There are people waiting for Eynar to bring the drinks for the unofficial
second meeting.

Every eye is on the pair. "Oh, shut up," says Eynar, behind the bar.
The yelllaughroaring is either an anchor or a speedthrowrolldriving wind.
He brings the drinks.

Darling's body

In her bunk wi Astrid lyan asleep, Darling thinks
aboot her body an whit sheu's waantid aa her life,

an whit sheu's gotten noo. Hid wisno ower haird,
aence sheu'd left her faithers' waant o corporate sons.

The maet o this transietion wis kent langsinsyne,
nae bother fer mosst o space, like jacks an limb extenders

an aa the bruck o bidan i'the varse, but sheu wis cursed
wi the wrang kinno faimly on the wrang kinno yird,

reclaimed fae regolith tae growe a fantasy
o pooer an no her awn confoodan sel. But noo,

Darling's body
    In her bedbunk with Astrid lying asleep, Darling thinks about her body
and what she's wanted all her life,
    and what she has now. It wasn't that hard, once she'd left her fathers'
wantneed of corporate sons.
    The foodmeat of this transition was long since known, no problem for
most of space, like jacks and limb extenders
    and all the rubbishscrap of waitstayliving in the universe, but she was
cursed with the wrong sort of family on the wrong sort of groundworldsoil,
    reclaimed from regolith to grow a fantasy of power and not her own
confounding self. But now,

happan her airms aroon her nesh body sheu's feart
sheu's draeman yet, that whit sheu's touchan wilno stey

whan sheu wakkens, a fossil fear as oot o time
as ony baest o ony presairve o Eart. Her body,

here, noo, shoudno be bidan in aald wirds,
but hid is. Unless – an this is the true an muckle fear –

whan Astrid's touchan her, whan Astrid casts a airm
ower her more-as-Martian skin. Whit maan it mean,

tae only ken thee body whan hid's wi anither?
An deus hid ivver mean onytheen ither as grief?

    wrapcoverbundling her arms around her softtenderhealing body she's
scared she's dreaming still, that what she's touching can't stay
    when she wakes, a fossil fear as out of time as any animalmonster of
any preserve of Earth. Her body,
    here, now, shouldn't be waitstayliving in old words, but it is. Except –
and this is the true and greatbig fear –
    when Astrid's touching her, when Astrid slings an arm across her
more-than-Martian skin. What must it mean,
    to only know your body when it's with another? And does it ever mean
anything other than grief?

Astrid canno draa yet

Hid isno that sheu isno
    makkan time. Even
        wi Darling, sheu's as faithfu

wi her slaets as faithless
    wi the kirk, an reglar
        as the yotun's spin.

But notheen comes at.
    Sheu's draan the full ring
        o the staetion, an sheu's draan

the peedie skiffs at sail
    atween hids ooter airms
        an substaetion bolas:

Astrid still can't draw

    It's not that she's not making time. Even with Darling, she's as faithful
    with her slates as faithless with the church, and regular as the gas
giant's spin.
    But nothing works out well. She's drawn the full ring of the station,
and drawn
    the little skiffs that sail between its outer arms and substation bolas:

but, puckle or muckle,
>   whither sheu's ramstam or huily,
>   whitivver hid is sheu's draan

hid's bruck. On Mars sheu caad
>   the shaeds o the yotun, the staens
>   o a meun, the dwangs o haem,

an wun the top mairks
>   an tutors' admieraetion.
>   Sheu canno leuk at yin noo.

An sheu wis nivver keen
>   on portraiture, but
>   this morneen sheu's wakkened aerly

in Darling's room abeun
>   the Hoose, an so sheu draas
>   the bonnie visietor sleepan.

but, grainsmall or greatbig, whether she's carelessheadstrongspeedy or carefulslowgentle, whatever it is she's drawn,
it's rubbishscrap. On Mars she callherded the colours of the gas giant, the stones of a moon, the struttoilstrains of home,
and won the top marks and tutors' admiration. She can't look at those now.
And she was never keen on portraiture, but this morning she's woken early
in Darling's room above the House, and so she draws the finepretty visitor asleep.

The aald exercises
            come tae her fingers
                        an noo sheu feels the glegness

sheu's missed aa this weeks.
            Astrid staps an pits
                        aside the sketch an draas

fae memory the islans
            o the Argyre Sea.
                        The more thir aesy an bonnie,

the more her uim growes,
            whill the traitor stylus
                        naeraboot snaps in her haand.

    The old exercises come to her fingers and she feels the
alertquickkeensmoothness
    she's missed all these weeks. Astrid stops and puts the sketch aside
and draws
    from memory the islands of the Argyre Sea. The more they are easy
and finepretty,
    the more her heatragemadness grows, until the traitor stylus nearly
snaps in her hand.

Gossip is Orcadia's craesh

thinks Margit, waatchan her smoosie bairn
    an Higgie the Codd both tell her aa
sheu needs tae ken an plenty sheu disno.
    Sheu smiles an offers twatree wirds
tae seem sheu's gien the sam as sheu's taen.
    Margit's played this gaem fer years,
an Gunnie's gey young tae ken the rules,
    an Higgie's gey aald tae bither noo.

Gossip is Orcadia's greasefat
    thinks Margit, watching her nosy child and Higgie the Coder both
tell her all she needs to know and plenty that she doesn't. She smiles and
offers a few words so it seems she's given the same as she's taken. Margit's
played this game for years, and Gunnie's pretty young to know the rules
and Higgie's pretty old to bother now.

Sheu drifts whan Gunnie reevles aboot
    Astrid an the toorist, fer yin
sheu saa hersel, an mibbe wis kent
    the meenit the pair o thaim landed. So whan
Higgie says, "Hid's no jeust me,"
    Margit disno ken whit sheu means.
But Higgie's untentie gittan, sheu haes
    a waant o tellan, a waant tae be haerd.

"Eynar is seen hid an aa, an Aslaug
    wadno spaek aboot hid, but
A'm haerd her offiece wis horrid messed
    on Thirday by. Hid's somtheen tae deu
wi the Lights. Wir seen. But dinno tell,"
    sheu says, more feart, gramsan thir airms.
"Dinno tell, fer I canno thole
    fock sayan A'm gyte." Her een is weet.

She drifts when Gunnie chatterprattles about Astrid and the tourist, because she'd seen that herself, and had probably known the minute they both landed. So when Higgie says, "It's not just me," Margit doesn't know what she means. But Higgie's become uncarefulwatchful, she wantneeds to tell, wantneeds to be heard.

"Eynar saw it too, and Aslaug wouldn't speak about it, but I heard her office was veryhorribly messed up last Thirdday. It's something to do with the Lights. We've seen. But don't tell," she says, more scared, snatchgrabbing their arms. "Don't tell, because I can't stand folk saying I'm crazy." Her eyes are wetrain.

Margit kens her meaneen. Affens
     fock say "dinno tell" tae say
"tell aabody, so I dinno hiv tae",
     but affens, "keep thee tong sneckid."
Margit kens whit wey hid is,
     an locks in Higgie's news wi ither
news sheu's lockid in, so sheu
     can lock in whar the meaneen bides.

     Margit knows what she means. Often, people say "don't tell" to mean
"tell everybody, so I don't have to", but often, "keep your tongue on the
latch." Margit knows whathowwherewhy it is, and locks in Higgie's news
with other news she's locked in, so she can lock in where the meaning
waitstaylives.

Gunnie Margitsbairn canno keep a secret

"Higgie's clean gyte," thay say. Brenna is soor
fae her failure at the Ting, an says,
"Sheu isno the only een. Erlend telt me
a uncan min in some sort o siller robb
speired him fer the time, an saantit, an Sigurd
saa tree fock like aalwarld cosmonaats,
flags an aa, chappan at his airlock,
an Auga says—" she disno tak a braeth
"—thir seean ships i'the rouk wi drives at isno
been invented." "Aye. Gyte," says Gunnie,
shakkan thir heid an sighan, aafil sad,
an Brenna says, "False consciousness." "Whit?"

Gunnie Margitschild can't keep a secret

"Higgie's gone completely crazy," they say. Brenna is
sourbitterrudemiserable from her failure at the Council, and says, "She's
not the only one. Erlend told me a strangerweird man in some sort of
silver robes asked him for the time, and spirited away, and Sigurd saw
three folk like old-world cosmonauts, flags and everything, knocking on
his airlock, and Auga says—" she doesn't draw breath "—they've seen
ships in the fogfrost with drives that haven't been invented." "Yes. Crazy,"
says Gunnie, shaking their head and sighing, veryawfully sad, and
Brenna says, "False consciousness." "What?"

"Thay canno right accept whit maan be deun,
so thir tellan taels instaed." "Yass, yass,
thir gyte." Gunnie gies her airm a dunt,
waantan tae haad hid, kennan sheu's raedy tae cup
intae her awn kinno ree, an naeraboot waantan
tae loup in ahint. Oot the screen, the spin
o Orcadia turns thaim tae the haaf, awey
fae the gowd leam o the yotun. The wynd mirkens.
"Hid's like thir waantan wir piece tae dee," says Brenna,
an Gunnie's bithert thirsel at that. "Na, na,"
thay say, ower quiet. "Thir jeust no sure
whit'll survive the chaenge." An the staetion birls.

    "They can't properly accept what must be done, and so they're
making up stories instead." "Yes, yes, they're crazy." Gunnie gives her
arm a shockchancestrike, wanting to hold it, knowing she's ready to
spilltip into her own kind of ragefuryfrenzy and nearly wantneeding
to jumpspringvault in behind. Through the screen, the spin of
Orcadia turns them to deep space, away from the golden glow of the
gas giant. The corridor enters twilight. "It's like they wantneed our
placedistancepartwhile to die," says Brenna, and Gunnie is worryirritated
at that. "No, no," they say, too quiet. "They just aren't sure what will survive
the change." And the station whirlrushdancespins.

Noor draems

Noor's quaaters is oot by the Hofn,
    a peedie cell by hidsel,
aneath the hulks sheu studies.
    The night thir a ring o Light
aroon her sleepeen kist
    wi no a body tae see it.
Sheu braethes; hid swaalls an birls;
    i'the mids o the wheel sheu draems.

Noor dreams

    Noor's quarters are out near the Havenharbour, a little cell on its own, beneath the hulks she studies. Tonight there's a ring of Light around her sleeping-chestcoffinbreast with no one there to see it. She breathes; it swellwaves and whirlrushdancespins; in the centre of the wheel she dreams.

The wracks is spaekan. Thir
        unfaaldan, a hingan glimro
o human wirds in waves
        atwart the shiftan waas:
equaetions, errows. A mooth
        appens wide i'the center
o the center. Hid spaeks; her haands
        grip, ungrip, grip.

Wi morneen, sheu's breeksed, hinkid
        i'the sheets like a bab or a corp,
sleepan yet whan sheu poors
        watter on poodered maet,
an sleepan whan sheu gaithers
        her notts an putters her skiff
oot tae the Wrack-Hofn.
        Hid's notheen ither as silent.

   The wrecks are speaking. They are unfolding, a hangleaning ghost-light
of human words in waves across the changedodgemoving walls: equations,
arrows. A mouth opens wide in the centre of the centre. It speaks; her
hands clench, unclench, clench.
   In the morning, she is exhausted, twisted in the sheets like a baby
or a corpse, sleeping still when she pours water on powdered foodmeat,
and sleeping when she gathers her notes and putters her skiff out to the
Wreck-Havenharbour. It's nothing other than silent.

But thir a calculaetion
     sheu canno shak, a nummer
tae remak the mynd o the meisurs.
     So noo sheu's back at the godssend,
hungered sam as this
     wir the first day on site,
whan nummers wirno been wrowt
     intae unmeanan an loss.

But there is a calculation she cannot shake, a number to remake the meaningmemorymindwill of the measurements. So now she's back at the salvagewrecktreasure, as hungry as if it were her first day on site, when numbers hadn't been worked into unmeaning and loss.

Darling catches wird fae haem

The bulletin's chaenged. Her faithers is chairted
her rodd a weys aroon the starns.
This wey. Whit wey deu thay ken? Whit nummers
is on the timer coontan doon?

Foo an birlan roon Wolf, mibbe
a body wis matched her face tae the caa,
her styman bletheran tae her face,
pitten her face an story taegither,

an cashed thaim in. That, or else
Autonomist ethics isno as geud
as thay claim. Whitivver wey: her faithers
ken tae ransel the inner Nord.

Darling catches word from home

The bulletin has changed. Her fathers have charted her route some
distance around the stars. This way. Whathowwherewhy do they know?
Which numbers are on the timer counting down?

Drunkmadfull and whirlrushdancespinning round Wolf, maybe
someone had matched her face to the callherd, her staggeringblinddrunk
talkchatrambling to her face, put her face and story together,

and cashed them in. That, or else Autonomist ethics aren't as good as
they claim. No matter how: her fathers know to searchsnoopransack the
inner North.

103

Noo the aafil grave quaistion:
tae bide in this coothie orbit, or git
enogh o a pin tae flit the sistem,
like a rogue comet? Agalis

fer peedie staens tae win tae escaep
velocity, an sheu's some tired,
an faimly's gotten ferfil weyght.
An here is Astrid, a body at's mibbe

growan anither gravity.
Tae bide, an hopp sheu's chaenged enogh
tae no be aesy clyped on tae
her faithers? An hopp whan thay come –

thay will, fer whit can gowd no deu –
thay'll no waant noo whit wey sheu is,
an hopp wi time enogh some wey
the Wheel'll no waant tae lat her gang?

Now the veryawfully serious question: to waitstaylive in this
friendlycomfortablepleasantunthreatening orbit, or to get enough
speedfeet to leaveflyescape the system, like a rogue comet? Extraordinarily
difficult
for little stones to reachtravelachieve escape velocity, and she's
very tired, and family is veryfearfully heavy. And here there's Astrid,
a personbody who is maybe
growing another gravity. To waitstaylive, and hope she's changed
enough to not be easily ratted out to her fathers? And hope when they
come –
they will, because what can't money do – they won't wantneed
whathowwherewhy she is, and hope with enough time somehow the
Wheel won't want to let her go?

104

Inga taks her yole oot

Sheu canno ask her crew tae wirk ony hairder,
or thole tae quyt whan sheu's taen in notheen
fer tree lang day: so here sheu is, alaen
abeun the swaall ithoot a keek o Light.
Sheu chairts the whirls, the lins, the mains an the birts
o the yallo yotun's flowan sphere, an whar
thay'll hopp tae find a sign o Lights the morn,
an than the osc stairts skrekkan like a bairn.

Inga takes her boat out

She can't ask her crew to work any harder, or stand to quit when
she's brought in nothing for three long days: so here she is, alone
above the swellwave without a peep of Light. She charts the whirls, the
restpauselulls, the main currents and the back currents of the yellow gas
giant's flowing sphere, and where they'll hope to find a sign of Lights
tomorrow, and then the oscilloscope starts yellscreeching like a child.

Inga kens sheu canno tak in the Lights
alaen, but: days ithoot a keek
an noo a mense o Light, the mosst fer months,
jeust whan sheu canno tak it. Sheu dives in,
intae the upper tides, intae the ee,
intae the ayebidan stoor o a stoor planet,
skittran atween helm, daikles an lines,
thraan a flyre atwart her luntit face.

Hid wisno possieble. Sheu shoud been wrackid.
Wi whit sheu did, Orcadia shoud been murnan
But luck o the fell gods is wi her (an yass,
sheu pits up a prayer a second anent the wind),
so whan at laast sheu docks at Lightness Bay,
weel by the turnan o the Stannart Day,
sheu's taen tae haem tree day or more o Light,
an sets aboot unloddan hid by hersel.

Inga knows she can't bring in the Lights by herself, but: days without a
peep and now a vast amount of Light, the most for months, just when she
can't take it. She dives in, into the upper seatimetides of gas, into the eye, into
the everlasting stormstrifestrainspeeddust of a stormstrifestrainspeeddust
planet, rushdarting about between helm, compasses and lines, twistthrowing
a leergrimace across her sparklightflaming face.

It wasn't possible. She should have been wrecked. With what she did,
Orcadia should have been mourning. But luck of the fiercecruelclever gods
is with her (and yes, she says a prayer a second againstaboutbefore the
wind), so when at last she docks at Lightness Hangar, well past the turning
of the Standard Day, she's brought to home three days or more of Light,
and starts to unload it by herself.

Astrid taks Darling tae a meun

Thay step intae a bruckit domm,
aa the poly taen fae the reuf,
an mosst o the dwangs an aa: liftid
back tae space tae big more bolas
an wheels whan the staetion wis growan.
Darling laens intae Astrid –
touchan trou seiven layers
o waakan claes – an leuks ap
at fower meuns. Or is it doon?
"I see why they gave up building here.
It's gorgeous but I'm sick already.
It's all too fast." "Faaster as whit?
Fock is movvan faaster on Mars,
relietive tae the centre." "But then
I couldn't see! And I stayed on the ground."

Astrid takes Darling to a moon

They step into a brokenrubbishruined dome, all the plasticpolymer
taken from the roof and most of the struttoilstrains as well: lifted back to
space to construct more bolas and wheels when the station was growing.
Darling leans into Astrid – touching through seven layers of spacewalk
clothes – and looks up at four moons. Or is it down? "I see why they gave
up building here. It's gorgeous but I'm sick already. It's all too fast." "Faster
than what? People move faster on Mars, relative to the centre." "But then
I couldn't see! And I stayed on the ground."

Sheu haps her airms aroon Astrid's waist
an kieks aff intae space. Thay flee
a fair piece. Thir tedders stretch.
Darling golders. Astrid, quiet,
flees thaim doon. "Dinno," sheu says.
"Fock dee that wey." "But we—" "Jeust ken,
fock dee. Jeust ken. Noo waatch." Orcadia
turns intae view, an the yotun,
an five, an sax more meuns. The tirlan
mathematics is a dose more
as Darling can compriehend, fer aa
sheu wis fower year sailan curves
closser tae the galactic centre.
Sheu kens, noo, hoo faast is faast,
an still, an hoo the staetion, spinnan,
pinned sicweys atween planet an starn,
the tree o thaim a godless grand
an trig triangle, faast an still,
is noo an aye the only rest.

She wrapcoverbundles her arms round Astrid's waist and kicks off
into space. They fly a good placedistancepartwhile. Their tethers stretch.
Darling yelllaughroars. Astrid, quiet, flies them down. "Don't," she says.
"People die that way." "But we—" "Just know, people die. Just know. Now
watch." Orcadia turns into view, and the gas giant, and five, and six more
moons. The turntwistwhirlspinning mathematics is far more than Darling
can comprehend, for all she was four years sailing curves closer to the
centre of the galaxy. She knows, then, how fastfixed is fastfixed, and
stillfixedsecretsilent, and how the station, spinning, pinned a specific
distance between planet and star, all three making a verygodless greatbig
and neatbriskcomplete triangle, fastfixed and stillfixedsecretsilent, is now
and always the only rest.

Tree

Astrid shaas Darling her wark

"It's beautiful!" says Darling. "Bonnie," sheu says,
cooriean in, giean a smuthick, no seean
the artist's teum leuk. "The yellows and greens,
the way you've caught the planetary winds.

How small the station seems in the corner. So much
feeling." Astrid canno spaek. Sheu spaeks:
"A'm no feelan hid." Darling laaghs.
"You might not know it but I think you are,

somewhere. Honestly, this is fantastic." The artist
wheenks an graabs her claes, waantan layers
atween her spacer skin an Darling's scunneran
enthusiasm. "Thoo disno unnerstaan."

Astrid showpasses Darling her work

"It's beautiful!" says Darling. "Finepretty," she says,
snugglenestlehuddling close, giving Astrid a kisscaresscuddle, missing
Astrid's emptyhungry look. "The yellows and greens, the way you've
caught the planetary winds.

How small the station seems in the corner. So much feeling." Astrid
can't speak. She speaks: "I don't feel it." Darling laughs. "You might not
know it but I think you are,

somewhere. Honestly, this is fantastic." The artist shrugtwitchflounces
off and grabs her clothes, wantneeding layers between her spacer skin and
Darling's sickspoilboring enthusiasm. "You don't understand."

Darling sees the ranyie noo, stairts
tae compriehend the scael o hid, her piece
in hid, the fear o hid. "Tell me?" But Astrid's
buskid an oot the doar, laevan her slaet.

Darling sees the writhingpain now, starts to comprehend the scale
of it, her placedistancepartwhile in it, the fear of it. "Tell me?" But Astrid's
dressprepared and has left, leaving her slate.

Inga is waantan pey

Whan Inga comes oot tae Noor
      tae pit a fingerprent
tae a slaet tae confirm the salvage –
      the credits tae be turst
intae the next shaef
      fer the next Autonomist ferry
tae tak tae a bankeen staetion,
      an fae thir furder oot
the gret galactic airm
      til hid wins tae a piece whar data
can traivel better an faaster
      by lang waves o light
as by a shaef on a ship,
      an twatree month hid'll be
afore a record comes back
      that on a muckle net

Inga is wantingwithout pay

When Inga comes out to Noor to put a fingerprint to a slate to confirm
the salvage – the credits to be trussbundlegrappled into the next sheafslice
for the next Autonomist ferry to take to a banking station, and from
there farther out the great galactic arm, until it reachtravelachieves the
placedistancepartwhile where data can travel better and faster by long
waves of light than by a sheafslice on a ship, and it will be a few months
before any record comes back that, on a greatbig net

o sairvers on some planet,
     a piece sheu'll nivver gang,
the nummers at track her credits
     is ap, an aence this process
teuk years, an inner staetions
     didno need credits,
but the less Orcadia maks
     the more hid's gotten nummers –
the arkaeolojist's sheuched
     in a bing o slaets an mummlan
uncan formulae,
     flippan fae slaet tae slaet.
"Thir a livveen in this?"
     speirs Inga. Noor turns.
Her een is a lightyear awey.
     "In what?" sheu says. An Inga

    of servers on a random planet, a placedistancepartwhile she'll never
go, the numbers that track her credits are up, and this process once took
years, and inner stations didn't need credits, but the less Orcadia makes
the more they have numbers – the archaeologist's burytrenchguttered in
a heapbin of slates and mumbling strangerweird formulae, flipping from
slate to slate. "Is there a living in this?" asks Inga. Noor turns. Her eyes are
a lightyear away. "In what?" she says. And Inga

waffs ower the blinkan gear,
      an, dootsome, oot the screen.
Noor cheeters. "In studying
      impenetrable galactic mysteries
without commercial use?"
      "Ya," says Inga, shruggan.
Noor, distracted, picks
      a slaet fer the docket.
"For now, but whims of funding
      might well summon me home
at any moment." Sheu leuks
      til a wrack. "Even now."
Hid's bobban on hids tedder.
      The spaekers bide silent.
The wrack laeves the screen.
      "Right enogh," says Inga.

signalgesturehintwaves at the flashingcursed equipment, and,
uncertain, through the screen. Noor chucklegiggles. "In studying
impenetrable galactic mysteries without commercial use?" "Yes," says Inga,
shrugging. Noor, distracted, tapchaptakes a slate for the docket. "For now,
though whims of funding might well summon me home at any moment."
She looks over at a wreck. "Even now." It's rockdanceswaying on its tether.
The speakers waitstaylive silent. The wreck leaves the screen. "I see," says
Inga.

"Me coseen is wi a college
          roon Alpha Centauri, wirkan
wi archives o 21st century
          intertextual narrative,
an sheu says somtheen like that.
          Right enogh. An if
more o thee fock cam in
          I doot thay'll be needan
fock at kens botts?"
          Noor sees the waant
i'the quaistion. Hid's the sam
          as the waant sheu's gotten whan fleean
roon wracks, the waant sheu's gramsan
          again: no jeust tae bide,
tae hae enogh maet tae bide,
          but tae bide wi uiss.

  "My cousin works at a college orbiting Alpha Centauri, working on
archives of 21st century intertextual narrative, and she says something like
that. OK then. And if more of your people travel here, I expect they will
need people who know boats?" Noor sees the wantneed in the question,
because it's the same wantneed she has had when flying around wrecks,
the wantneed she's snatchgrabbing again: not just to waitstaylive, to have
enough foodmeat to waitstaylive, but to waitstaylive with use.

Sheu shaas the salvage docket
        tae Inga. "Here," sheu says,
an "If . . ." The yolewife waits.
        "If what I think I've found . . ."
Noor shaks her heid an fires
        a queek peedie freesk.
"I'll ask," sheu says. The wracks
        pass by. "I'll certainly ask."

She showpasses the salvage docket to Inga. "Here," she says, and
"If . . ." The boat worker waits. "If what I think I've found . . . " Noor shakes
her head and chuckthrowfires a quick little false smile. "I'll ask," she says.
The wrecks pass by. "I will certainly ask."

117

Darling peys Olaf fer a hurl

"I'm interested," sheu says, "in how you work."
Olaf is dozent, hingan atween blaetness,
twartieness an his awn restless virr
fer the botts an the Lights. He kinno waants tae tell
ivrytheen tae sombody, but disno
ken whit like a body sheu is, but
is fyarmt, but disno waant tae disappoynt,
but is prood, but is feart, so says,
"Oh yaas," lukkan oot, an notheen more.
The yole sails oot the dock wi ferfil quiet.

Darling pays Olaf for a tripspeedride
   "I'm interested," she says, "in how you work." Olaf is stymiestupefied,
hangleaning between shynessdiffidence, perverse grumpiness and his own
restless vigourwhirr for the boats and the Lights. He sort of wantneeds to
tell everything to someone, but doesn't know what sort of someone she
is, but is flattercajoled, but doesn't want to disappoint, but is proud, but is
afraid, so says, "Mhm," looking out, and nothing more. The boat sails out of
the dock, veryfearful quiet.

Darling's peyed him, tho, an wisno borned
tae walth or comed atwart the galaxy
ithoot lairnan somtheen aboot tisan
a faevor: sheu leuks fer less o the suspiecion
an more o the desire. Sheu speirs him slaa
an huily, piece an piece, laevan space
tae leuk at space, draas oot a bit o wittans,
here an thir, on hoo tae steer an hoo
tae leuk an whit tae waatch an whar tae ken
the gret yotun's dose o daenjers bide.

Darling has paid him, though, and wasn't born to wealth or come
across the galaxy without learning something about coaxcajoling a favour:
she looks for less of the suspicion and more of the desire. She questions
him laxslow and carefulslowgentle, bit by bit, leaving space to look at
space, draws out a little wisdomknowledgenews, here and there, on how to
steer and how to look and what to watch and where to know the great gas
giant's many dangers waitstaylive.

So whan Olaf says "Whit i'the naem . . ."
an draps the drive o the yole tae a tentie putter,
sheu disno speir right awey an disno mak
a panshite, but leuks oot whar he leuks an waits.
Abeun the yotun afore them the Lights is biggan
a face. Thir isno anither wird. I'the rouk
thir twatree thoosan poynts o Light biggan
a face the size o a meun: aald, aald,
lang beard, ae ee appen, ae ee puckered,
ae mooth appen, appen an rashan forrit.

So when Olaf says, "What in the name . . ." and drops the drive of the
boat to a carefulwatchful putter, she doesn't ask right away and doesn't
cause a panicfussflurry, but looks out where he looks and waits. Above the
gas giant before them the Lights are building a face. There's no other word.
In the fogfrost there are several thousand points of Light building a face
the size of a moon: old, old, long beard, one eye open, one eye puckered,
one mouth open, open and rushraining forward.

120

The god swallaes the yole. Aa's dairk: nae light,
nae Lights. A notion o speed, o weyght, an than—
thay spret intae the starns, oot the pug
o the planet. Olaf's screens bleusk, blue,
sproot, staedy. He haals thaim intae orbit
ahint Orcadia. Darling's grip relaxes:
sheu's cloort her saet's shinan aald black poly,
ten white lines doon aither side. Sheu hoasts.
"That doesn't usually happen?" sheu says, ithoot
a moot o a smile, an Olaf replies, "Na."

The god swallowdrinks the boat. All is dark: no light, no Lights.
The ideaexperimentinvention of speed, of weight, and then— they
startstripburstjump into the stars, out of the belly of the planet.
Olaf's screens flash, blue, sparkspit, steady. He hauls them into orbit
behind Orcadia. Darling's grip relaxes: she's clawscratched her seat's
shining old black plasticpolymer: ten white lines down either side. She
coughharrumphclears. "That doesn't usually happen?" she says, without
a hintwhisper of a smile, and Olaf says, "Nope."

Astrid speirs her faither fer advice

Thay spaek aboot his years o relatievistic
speed, haalan bits o Wheels an Light
atween Mars an the inner staetions: the distance,
the thrill, the kinno fock on langship freighters,
the needle o haem. Twinty-fower year:
twa return trips, than a stop. A freighter's
a puckle o fock an a demption o noyse, but no
a histry, an that wey isno that far fae paece.

Astrid asks her father for advice

   They speak about his years of relativistic speed, hauling pieces of
Wheels and Light between Mars and the inner stations: the distance,
the thrill, the types of people on longship freighters, the needle of home.
Twenty-four years, two return trips, then a stop. A freighter's a few people
and an inundation of noise, but not a history, and being like that is not
very far from peace.

Thay spaek aboot Orcadia's histry, the thraan
mixter-maxter o fock at biggid the staetion,
the trachle tae cheuss anither wey o cheussan,
the hunder o year o bean a piece at fock
fae grander pieces cam fer somepiece ither,
the fock at steyed, the fock at flit. The chaenges.
Whit isno chaenged. Whit shoudno. Whit might. Whit maan.
Whit will. The speed at's noo catcht up wi thaim.

Thay spaek aboot Mars. The trang o the surface. Aboot
the weyght o a planet. Aboot hoo a starn leuks
fae ither starns. Aboot whit thir seen an Inga
isno. Aboot whit Inga kens fae nivver
laevan an whit fae laevan thay'll nivver ken.
Thay dinno spaek aboot Darling ava, an thay dinno
spaek aboot art, an thay dinno spaek aboot whither
Astrid's bidan haem or no. But thay deu.

They speak about Orcadia's history, the tossedawkward mix of people
that built the station, the drudgemuddletrudge to choose a different way
of choosing, the hundreds of years of being a placedistancepartwhile that
people from greatbigger placedistancepartwhiles went to go somewhere
else, the people that stayed, the people that leaveflyescaped. The changes.
What hasn't changed. What shouldn't. What might. What must. What
will. The speed that's now caught up with them.
    They speak about Mars. The crowdbustlecloseness of the surface.
About the weight of a planet. About how a star looks from other stars.
About what they've seen and Inga hasn't. About what Inga knows from
never leaving and what from leaving they'll never know. They don't speak
about Darling at all, and they don't speak about art, and they don't speak
about Astrid waitstayliving home or not. But they do.

Darling gies Eynar the tael

"And then the face just spat us out!"
Sheu's smilan wide at the tig o daeth.
"Olaf steered us home safe,
but wouldn't say another word,

as if the Light had taken his tongue."
Eynar haads her glentan een.
"Fine tael," he says, an notheen more.
"Oh, come on!" Sheu's aafil fasht.

"It's more than a tale. And I know we're not
the only ones. I heard—" "Whit
did thoo hear?" Darling spys the danger
this time. "Oh," sheu says, "Just

Darling tells Eynar the story

"And then the face just spat us out!" She's smiling wide at the taptwitchtease of death. "Olaf steered us home safe, but wouldn't say another word,

like the Light had taken his tongue." Eynar holds her glinting eyes. "Good story," he says, and nothing more. "Oh, come on!" She's veryawfully fussvexworried.

"It's more than a story. And I know we're not the only ones. I heard—" "What did you hear?" Darling seespots the danger this time. "Oh," she says, "Just

that other folk had seen strange things.
That folk are talking." "Aye weel," he says,
"fock spaek a lot o guff." An he gangs
tae the back reum, whar surely thir wark.

Darling leuks aboot her. Thir
a puckle o fock i'the Hoose. "It's not
just me," sheu says tae naebody. "I know
you've seen them too." Thir no a reply.

that other people had seen strange things. That folk are talking." "Yes,
well," he says, "people say a lot of stinkpuffsnortnonsense." And he heads
to the back room, where there's surely work.

Darling looks around. There are a few people in the House. "It's not
just me," she says to no one. "I know you've seen them too." There's no
reply.

The Dance

Aence, the fock at first cam here
kent a planet's elliptiecal orbit,
seasons an a almanac,
Noo thir cruisies an year-roond wark.

But thay keepid the aalwarld time,
an cruisies is set tae Stannart Days,
whitivver thir staetion's spin. Thir dances,
preens tae string the yearless year.

So Brenna and Higgie is stringan a line
atwart the Haa wi light-ap letters,
in a tong thay deu an dinno spaek,
spellan oot "Harvest Home".

The Dance

Once the people who first came here knew a planet's elliptical orbit, seasons and an almanac. Now they have sun-lamps and year-round work.

But they kept the old world's time, and sun-lamps are set to Standard Days, whatever their station's spin. There are dances, pins along which to string the yearless year.

So Brenna and Higgie are stringing a line across the Hall with light-up letters, in a tongue they do and don't speak, spelling out "Harvest Home".

Ither fock redd an sweep the floar.
Eynar is biggan a bar i'the corner.
On stage, the band is checkan tuins
wi haand-held sinths an tings tae bang,

an a hollow body o wid an wire
at's played fer twatree hunder o year,
ower wi fock on a aerly ship.
The soond thay mak taegither is wyld.

~

Afore the dance, thir bairns unnaemed.
Astrid explaens the service tae Darling:
at seiven or eyght Stannart Year,
whan raedy an chossen, thay tak a naem –

Other people clear and sweep the floor. Eynar is building a bar in the
corner. On stage, the band is checking tunes with hand-held synths and
things to bang,
and a hollow body of wood and wire that's played for a few hundred
years, come here with people on a ship early on. The sound they make
together is wild.
~
Before the dance, there's the unnamed children. Astrid explains the
service to Darling: at seven or eight Standard Years, when they're ready
and have chosen, they take a name –

127

or, in Orcadia's wirds, gie –
a naem an a sel tae the staetion's care.
Thir tree the night, an parents an elders,
an ither fock at choss tae waatch,

like Darling, stannan at the back.
This year hid's Øyvind's taen the role
o Naemer. He haads a gless o bleud.
(Hid's sinthesised, no oot o shaem,

but bleud o a lamb is ower rare
an ower dear this lang weys in.)
Erlendsbairn hitches thir sark,
steps apae the aald wid altar

an harks in Øyvind's lug. The Naemer
draas a ring on the bairn's broo,
haads skinnymalinky airms, an cries,
"Haelga!" Sheu steps doon. An "Haelga!"

or, in Orcadia's words, give – a name and a self to the station's care.
There are three tonight, along with their parents and elders, and people
that chose to watch,

like Darling, standing at the back. This year Øyvind has taken the
role of Namer. He holds a glass of blood. (It's synthesised, not because
of shame

but because the blood of a lamb is too rare and too expensive such a
long distance into the galaxy.) Erlendsbairn lifts up the hem of their shirt,
steps up to the old wood altar,

and whisperwishes in Øyvind's ear. The Namer draws a ring on the
child's forehead, holds very skinny arms, and callnameproclaims, "Haelga!"
She steps down. And "Haelga!"

cries the crood, hintan the naem.
Darling's voyce is brakkan noo.
Sheu speirs o Astrid – a seicont bairn
steps ap – "But what if she's got it wrong?"

Astrid's a bittie bombazed. "Thir aye
anither year," sheu says, grabbid.
Darling's een is wheels. "How often
are you allowed to take a name?"

Astrid: "Wheesht!" The naem comes: "Kit!"
"Thir nae a rule," sheu mummles, thight.
Darling thinks fer a peedie blink.
"Could I give a name?" sheu speirs, saft.

Astrid disno reply, an waatches
the laast o the bairns spaek tae the Naemer:
Erikasbairn, sibleen o Brenna.
Øyvind stairts whan he hears the naem.

    callnameproclaims the crowd, gathergleansnatching her in. Darling's
voice is breaking now. She asks Astrid – the second child steps up – "But
what if she's got it wrong?"
    Astrid's a little bewilderstupified. "There's always another year," she
says, vexed. Darling's eyes are wheels. "How often are you allowed to take
a name?"
    Astrid: "Shush!" The name comes: "Kit!" "There's no rule," she
mumbles, tight-lipped. Darling thinks for a little blankblink. "Could I give
a name?" she asks, softgentlestupid.
    Astrid doesn't reply, and watches the last child speak to the Namer:
Erikasbairn, sibling of Brenna. Øyvind starts when he hears the name.

A still. "Astrid!" he cries, an Astrid
hears the Haa cry oot her naem,
kennan hid isno fer her, but thinkan
some wey yet hid shuirly is.

~

The dance begins. The band gits gaan,
neesteran at first like a injine sat
fer a year, but seun enogh runnan
fine. Thir leader caas the dance:

a tree-step first, tae rax oot limbs
an find the yivver feet thir baet
an dancers thir pairtners; next a set
tae frapp thaim ap, an than a waaltz.

A pauselullsecretsilence. "Astrid!" he callnameproclaims, and Astrid
hears the Hall callnameproclaim her name, knowing that it's not for her,
but thinking that somehow it surely is.

~

The dance begins. The band gets going, snortcreaksqueaking at first
like an engine left to sit for a year, but soon enough running well. Their
leader calls out the names and steps of the dances:

a three-step first, to stretchreachexpand out limbs and for
eagershakeanxious feet to find their beat, and for dancers to find their
partners; then a set-dance, tae mixtangle them up, and then a waltz.

Darling waants tae be the first
tae the floar. But Astrid haads her back,
mibbe oot o waantan tae see
the aalder folk's exemple first,

mibbe more oot o fear, or jeust
a curn o shaem. But wi the waaltz
sheu finds hersel an lifts her Darling
ontae the floar. Thir plenty wi thaim.

~

Eynar's waatchan fae ahint his bottles
fer Noor tae come. He disno show hid.
He disno ken hoo he's bithert, or mibbe
he deus: he's mibbe no gaan tae see

Darling wants to be the first to the floor. But Astrid holds her back,
maybe out of wantneeding to see the old people's example first,

maybe more out of fear, or just a motegrain of shame. But with the
waltz she finds herself and lifts Darling up to the floor. There are plenty of
people with them.

~

Eynar's watching from behind his bottles for Noor to come. He doesn't
show it. He doesn't know why he's worried about it, or maybe he does:
maybe he's not going to see

anither dance, an waants tae dance
wi a new body at'll mak a meaneen.
He smiles at Olaf wi his bairn,
liftan thaim an birlan roond,

an at the new-naemed youngsters dansan
aafil solemn, tentie noo
as aalder fock, but ithoot age's
grace an sprets o scarsome speed.

An at the pairtners, futurs telt
i'the wey o thir grip: ower closs
or ower lowse or glydan by
wi the aese o binary starns. (Ya, but

another dance, and wants to dance with a new bodyperson who'll
make a meaning. He grins at Olaf with his child, lifting them and
whirlrushdancespinning round,
    and at the new-named youngsters dancing veryawfully solemn,
carefulwatchful now as the old people, but without age's grace and
startstripburstjumps of terrifying speed.
    And at the partners, futures toldwarned in how they hold each other:
too close or too loose or gliding by with the ease of binary stars. (Yes, but

thir aye anither body coman
on anither curve tae mak
a fankelt problem, an best kens
whit wey the calculaetions come.)

~

Noor isno coman. Sheu's at the Hofn,
alaen, no myndan, mummlan nummers,
testan oot equaetions, rypan
the mosst obscure o airticles

i'the laest reputable o jurnals
fer ivry uncan formula
tae shape aroon the shape o the wracks.
Ayont her een the Lights is gaitheran;

there's always another bodyperson coming on another curve to make a
puzzletangled problem, and gods know whathowwherewhy the calculation
will come out.)

~

Noor isn't coming. She's at the Havenharbour, alone, not
rememberknowreflectwilling, mumbling numbers, testing equations,
searchplundercleardigging the most obscure articles
    in the least reputable journals for every strangerweird formula to
shape around the shape of the wrecks. Out of her eyeline the Lights are
gathering;

ahint her, paitrens sheu canno see.
Sheu's pittan her haands tae the black waas:
no clift tae rive at or kneb tae press,
but sheu's pressan, room by room.

Pick that, feel this, kick yin, caam doon.
Nivver kens sheu hoo desire is comed,
or if hid'll faa intae notheen again.
Sheu bides wi the draem an no wi time.

~

Thir dance is oot the ither side
o night, the cruisies giean the wynds
a dairker reid fer gangan haem.
But plenty's left fer dansan yet.

behind her, patterns she can't see. She's putting her hands on the black walls: without a crackchink to wrenchripbreak at or knobbeakpointbutton to press, but she's pressing, room by room.

Tapchaptake that, feel this, kick that, calm down. She doesn't know why desire has come, or if it'll fall into nothing again. She waitstaylives with the dream and not with time.

~

Their dance has come out the other side of night, the sun-lamps giving the corridors a darker red for going home. But there's plenty of time left for dancing.

134

Gunnie becks tae Higgie wi aa
the coortesy o young tae aald.
Thay whip her awey. Brenna's taen
her sleepan sister oot fer a waaltz.

Inga an Øyvind is comed in late
tae hae the virr fer the best o the dance:
fock drucken an lipperan wi haanless joy.
Thir steps an skips is naet an queek,

birlan each ither wi weel-kent airms.
Olaf an Erlend tummle afore thaim:
thay loup the footers no brakkan thir baet.
Øyvind wis taen ower lang tae win haem

Gunnie curtseybows to Higgie with all the courtesy of young to old.
They gustdarttwistattack her off. Brenna's taken her sleeping sister out for
a waltz.

Inga and Øyvind came late to have enough vigourwhirr for the best of
the dance: people drunk and fullspilloverflowing with clumsyuseless joy.
Their steps and skips are neat and quick,

whirlrushdancespinning each other with familiar arms. Olaf and
Erlend tumble in front of them: they jumpspringvault the clumsy fools
without breaking their beat. Øyvind had taken too long to reach home,

fae ooter space, an Inga wis born
an wun ages wi him in his final run,
but thay aye coud dance. Thay hurl
doon the Haa's muckle set.

~

But Darling an Astrid isno thir.
Thir comed oot the back o the Haa tae a bell
tae braethe an waatch anither stoor,
the Lights' antics in time wi the meusic.

Anunder the glamour Darling speirs
again: "Could I take a name?" An Astrid
turns. "We gie. But thoo – tae wha?
Wha kens thee enogh tae gie hid back?

    from outer space, and Inga was born and grew up to his age during his
final run, but they always could dance. They speedthrowrolldrive down the
Hall's greatbig set.

~

    But Darling and Astrid aren't there. They've come out to the
back of the Hall to a bubblebell to breathe and watch another
stormstrifestrainspeeddust, the Lights' antics in time with the music.
    Under the magicdelight Darling asks again, "Could I take a name?" And
Astrid turns. "We give. But you – to who? Who knows you enough to give
it back?

Thoo canno jeust tak whit thoo waants." "What I need,"
says Darling, wi peedie voyce, but this
is warse. "Yin's whit I sayed," spits Astrid,
een reflectan the skyran Lights.

Darling isno deualess. Wi feck,
sheu pelters Astrid. Sheu naems the dreids
at Astrid thinks is darnt but lie
ower closs tae the skin. Sheu fires:

"Just because you lost your home,
doesn't mean the rest of us
can't look for ours," an "Some of us never
had a piece." The wird is cruel.

You can't just take what you wantneed." "What I need," says Darling,
with a little voice, but this is worse. "That's what I said," spits Astrid, eyes
reflecting the gaudyshining Lights.

Darling's not feebleuseless. With powerworthattention, she
pelthammerruns Astrid. She names the dreads that Astrid thinks are
hidenestled but which lie too close to the skin. She chuckthrowfires:

"Just because you lost your home, doesn't mean the rest of us can't look
for ours," and "Some of us never had a placedistancepartwhile." The word
is cruel.

"You can't understand what it's like, to free
yourself from all this expectation,
to have to remake yourself." Is Darling
listened tae notheen o Astrid's haem?

Or ower much? Sheu isno telt
enogh o her life tae fer this tae laand
ither as cruel, her waants fankled
i'the voyce o pouer. So Astrid plays

the dour local, sayan notheen,
turnan awey, an noo hid's Darling
at's peltran doon the set's centre,
the dancers aesy sweengan by.

~

"You can't understand what it's like, to free yourself from all this
expectation, to have to remake yourself." Has Darling listened to nothing
of Astrid's home?

Or too much? She hasn't said enough about her life for any of this to
land any other way than cruel, her wantneeds tanglepuzzled with the voice
of power. So Astrid plays

the dour local, saying nothing, turning away, and now it's Darling
that's pelthammerrunning down the centre of the set, the dancers easily
swinging to let her by.

~

Thir jeust the ae dance noo: a waaltz.
The dancers is breeksed. A few can leuk
in thir pairtners' een, but mosst is jeust
heids on shudders an shucklan feet.

Thir ither fock in uncan claes,
an Light is gaitheran roon the girders.
Aabody's on the floar, no seean,
or mibbe thir seean an irno fasht.

A airy pair in oo waaltz roon
a see-trou pair in poly, a treesome
in cotton gang trou a fowersome in siller.
Roon an trou, ganfer or maet

There's only one dance left now: a waltz. The dancers are
exhaustedbroken. A few are able to look into their partners' eyes, but most
are only heads on shoulders and shufflelimping feet.

There are other people in strangerweird clothes, and Light is gathering
round the girders. Everybody's on the floor, not seeing, or maybe they're
seeing and don't care.

An airy pair in wool waltz round a transparent pair in plasticpolymer,
a threesome in cotton go through a foursome in silver. Round and through,
ghostomen or foodmeat

or light or Light: dancers dansan.
Is hid meusic? Whit body movs
whit body's body? Roon an trou,
maan feet write answers on the floar?

~

The fock o the staetion gang oot the doar.
Eynar an Margit is rotad on cleanan.
Thay sweep an swabble an dight oot the Haa.
An eftir, Eynar taks a sit.

"Did thoo see yin?" Sheu sits hersel.
"Did thoo no?" An Eynar nods.
"Thinks thoo will we see hid again?" he speirs,
like a bairn. "A'll no," sheu says. "We might."

or light or Light: dancers dancing. Is there music? What personbody
moves what personbody's personbody? Round and through, must feet
write answers on the floor?

~

The people of the station leave. It's Eynar and Margit's turn to clean.
They sweep and swillmop and cleanwipe out the Hall. And after, Eynar sits
down.
"Did you see that?" She sits down. "Didn't you?" And Eynar nods.
"Do you think we'll see it again?" he asks, like a child. "I won't," she says.
"We might."

Gunnie an Brenna imajin futures

Thir cooried in Gunnie's reum
the eftirneun eftir the dance:
thir no left yet. A day

fer raxan, rowan an restan
the both o thir bodies. Her haand
in thir hair, thir heid on her chest,

Gunnie thinks on thir waants.
A piece wi thir mither, yass,
but a yole o thir awn wad be better.

Inga's ower wabbit:
thir livveens tae be gotten,
wi a puckle o chaenges.

Gunnie and Brenna imagine futures

They're snugglenestlehuddled in Gunnie's room the afternoon after
the dance: they haven't left yet. A day
    for stretchreachexpanding, rolling and resting both of their bodies.
Her hand in their hair, their head on her chest,
    Gunnie thinks about what they wantneed. A placedistancepartwhile
with their mother, yes, but a boat of their own would be better.
    Inga's too tiredbroken: there are livings to be had, with a few changes.

Brenna can hiv her races
tae Federal Tings, as lang's
sheu taks back better daels;

fer aa her haivers sheu kens
gowd an refuses tae quyt.
Yaas, thir aye a wey.

Fer her pairt, Brenna is slippan
fae ae draem tae the tither,
fae crisis tae revolution.

In waarm wakkan, sheu
thinks on organisan
an reorganisan,

coories closser, fer in
this theoretiecal bed
thir futures tae be maed.

Brenna can have her trips to the Federal Councils, as long as she brings
back better deals;
for all her noisy nonsense she knows about money and refuses to quit.
Yes, there's always a way.
For her part, Brenna is slipping from one dream to the next, from crisis
to revolution.
In warm waking, she thinks about organising and reorganising,
snugglenestlehuddles closer, because in this theoretical bed there are
futures to be made.

Astrid, oot

A peedie beeteen's needed
on a peedie module oot
the end o Aikeray:

a Papa, monietoran
micro-waith, the driv
o scows at murder-speeds

passan ivry oor.
Ithoot defense, the staetion
wad be wrackid in seconds.

Astrid needed oot
her heid, so teuk a wark
fae the Ting's duty-boards.

Astrid, out

A little repairpaintimprovement is needed on a small module attached
to the far end of Aikeray:

a Papa, monitoring micro-debris, the rainshower of fragmentruins
travelling at murder-speeds

passing every hour. Without defence, the station would be wrecked in
seconds.

Astrid needed to get out of her head, so took a job from the Council's
duty-boards.

143

The repair wis coman at.
Thay uissed this kinno wark
tae lairn bairns the staetion.

The wrench kens her haand.
Her haand kens the turn.
Aroon her is a murgis

o starns an instruments,
but Astrid keeps her een
on the haand, the wrench, the wark.

Wi ivry rive her hairt
is ruggid furder appen.
Ony tear wad bide

The repair was progressing. They used this sort of work to teach children about the station.

The wrench knows her hand. Her hand knows the turn. Around her is a riotcrowdmud

of stars and instruments, but Astrid keeps her eyes on the hand, the wrench, the work.

With every wrenchripbreak her heart is teargnawknotted further open. Any tear would waitstaylive

at the buddom o her mask
til sheu wis back inbye,
an so sheu disno greet.

Beeteen deun sheu lies,
mask tae the metal,
braethan wi the staetion.

at the bottom of her mask until she was back inside, and so she doesn't weep.

Repairpaintimprovement done she lies, mask to the metal, breathing with the station.

Darling meets Margit Lighter fer bisness

Sheu isno spokken tae Astrid
fae the dance twa day by,
but sheu's maed ap her mynd.
Sheu wis maed ap her mynd i'the mids
o the cangle, the meenit sheu ran,
wi ivry ee on her back.
Yestreen sheu wis gotten a meeteen
wi Margit tae mak the proposal;

Darling meets Margit the Lighter for business

She hasn't spoken to Astrid since the dance two days ago, but she's made up her mind. She had made up her mind in the middle of the argumentwrangling, the moment she ran, with every eye on her back. Yesterday she had a meeting with Margit to make the proposal;

the day thay'll shak haands.
Sheu's sat at the waa o the bay,
waatchan twatree yoles
laanchan fer the yotun,
whan Margit waffs a haand
afore her. "Whar wir thoo!"
"Out there," says Darling, poyntan
trou the containment dyke.

"Thir time fer that," says Margit.
Sheu's blide. Darling didno
think that sheu'd be blide.
Sheu wis jubish, than ootward, noo blide.
Whan Darling's Martian naem
is pitten tae the chit,
sheu's happier yet. "Dinno fash,"
says the ex-yolewife.

today they'll shake hands. She's sitting against the wall of the
hangar, watching a few boats launching for the gas giant, when Margit
signalgesturehintwaves a hand in front of her. "Where were you!" "Out
there," says Darling, pointing through the containment wallfieldbarrier.
    "There's time for that," says Margit. She's happyfondpleased
and Darling didn't think she'd be happyfondpleased. She was
suspiciousanxiousdoubtful, then outwardreserveddistant, now
happyfondpleased. When Darling's Martian name is put to the chit, she's
even more happy. "Don't fussvexworry," says the ex-boat worker.

"A'll no tell a sowel.
Credits peys fer quiet.
Kens thoo whit thoo're deuan?"
"No yet. I'll learn." "Hid's chancy."
"I've seen. I'd like to see more."
"Thoo kens the Lights is chaengan."
Darling's surprised tae hear
a body admit hid. Tae her.

"I ken. And maybe that's what
I want to see. I'll learn."
"Thoo will." Margit is siccar.
"What will you do?" An Margit's
dairk een lowe.
Sheu's tree times Darling's age
but noo seems younger.
"Bairn," sheu says, "whit'll I no?"

    "I won't tell a soul. Credits pay for quiet. Do you know what you're
doing?" "Not yet. I'll learn." "It's riskyunlucky." "I've seen. I'd like to see
more." "You know the Lights are changing." Darling's surprised to hear
someone admit it. To her.
    "I know. And maybe that's what I want to see. I'll learn." "You will."
Margit is stableseveresteadfast. "What will you do?" And Margit's dark
eyes flameglowflickerflare. She's three times Darling's age, but now seems
younger. "Child," she says, "what won't I do?"

Eynar pits oot a advert

But Eynar writan his wirds leuks grim.
"Bar", hid raeds. "Going Concern."
He checks his skeulbeuk. "Get Away
From It All. Opportunity
For Fantastic Growth." He adds
exclamaetion mairks, than hits
delete. He adds a dose o hashtags
an thinks on wha might sairch thaim oot.

Eynar sends out an advert
But Eynar writing his words looks grimgrey. "Bar", it reads. "Going
Concern." He checks his textbook. "Get Away From It All. Opportunity For
Fantastic Growth." He adds exclamation marks, then hits delete. He adds
a lot of hashtags and thinks about who might search for them.

The text's gaan oot tae the center o tings:
Alpha Centauri, than Sol, fer Mars.
An than fae thir back intae the haaf.
Muckle orbital fock first,
than muckle grunders wi fantasies
o fock like him. Than peedier pieces,
peedier fock at canno thole
thir haem an canno thole a dreef.

Can Eynar thole a dreef? Weel,
he's time. Months, likely, aye,
afore thir ony replies. Can aye
chaenge his mynd. He leuks aboot
his Hoose, hids chairs an taebles, waas
hung wi viddies, print-oots, bruck.
He pits a simpler message tae Noor:
"Coman oot. Waant onytheen?"

The text is heading out to the centre of things: Alpha Centauri, then Sol, for Mars. And then from there back into deep space. Biggreat orbital people first, then biggreat planet-dwellers with fantasies about people like him. Then littler placedistancepartwhiles, littler people who can't stand their home and can't stand a crowdherd.

Can Eynar stand a crowdherd? Well, he has time. Months, likely, yes, before there are any replies. Can always change his mind. He looks around his House, its chairs and tables, walls hung with video screens, print-outs, rubbishscrap. He sends a simpler message to Noor: "Coming out. Do you wantneed anything?"

Stoor

The yotun is still whan thay laanch, or seems
still: hids swaalls o gas more gless
as birlan wind. But fae this distance
wind is apaece an fire is caald.

So eftir jeust a day o rest,
Inga, Olaf an the tree o thir crew,
breeksed yet fae the muckle dance,
sail the rouk in sairch o Light.

Øyvind choss the kirk an no
the laancheen bay, preferran prayer
tae seean them aff: an aald wint
he thowt he'd tint at ruggid him

Stormduststrife

The gas giant is stillfixedsecretsilent when they launch, or
seems stillfixedsecretsilent: its swellwaves of gas more glass than
whirlrushdancespinning wind. But from this distance, wind is stillpeaceful
and fire is cold.

So after only one day of rest, Inga and Olaf and all three of their crew,
still exhaustedbroken from the greatbig dance, sail the fogfrost in search
of Light.

Øyvind chose the church and not the launch hangar, preferring prayer
to seeing them off, an old habitcustompractice he thought he'd lost that
teargnawknotted him

the day: some imp o fear demandan
his holy time an holy wirds.
He asks the gods tae mynd thaim on.
He nivver asks fer ower much.

Whan Inga sails an Øyvind prays,
teddert tae the staetion's tide,
a play o Lights noo taks tae tirlan
i'the yotun's brist an hoved hairt.

~

Higgie's deep i'the codd whan thay sail,
an deeper yet whan the screens ahint
is stairtan tae shaa the aerly signs
o a mortal stoor. Sheu caas the bays.

today: some devil of fear demanding his holy time and holy words.
He asks the gods to rememberknowreflectwill them. He never asks for
very much.

As Inga sails and Øyvind prays, tethered to the station's seatimetide,
a play of Lights begins turntwistwhirlspinning in the gas giant's
squeezepressbruised and swollenrisen heart.

~

Higgie's deep in code when they sail, and deeper still when
the screens behind start showing the early signs of a deathly
stormstrifestrainspeeddust. She calls the hangars.

Thay'll send alairm tae ivry yole
tae come back in. She pits up a wird.
Sheu's deun whit sheu can deu. An than
her awn alairm begins tae skrek

an ivry screen at aence aizes
in error-light, an afore sheu can see
whit's whit a muckle root braks
fae the deck o the plant. Sheu rins tae see.

The faalds o pouer aroon the bots
is buljan an thratchan like a seck
o rattans, refractors an connectors
lipperan wi light, ivry een.

They will send alarm to every boat to come back in. She prays. She's
done what she can do. And then her own alarm begins to yellscreech
    and every screen at once blazes in error-light, and before she can see
what's what a greatbig roarbellow breaks from the floor of the plant. She
runs to see.
    The fieldstrandfolds of power around the machines are bulging and
writhing like a sack of rats, refractors and connectors overflowing with
light, each one.

Whan sheu draps her hand, the Lights
is maed a spinnan triple helix
i'the plant's center. Sheu canno hear
alairms noo. Sheu only waatches.

~

Darling's at the bays fer the laanch,
seean hoo hid's deun. Sheu's thinkan
on tellan Astrid aboot the yole.
Will hid haad her, or gar her gang?

Darling kens whit future sheu waants,
but aither wey's a future. An than
Higgie's waarneen o the stoor comes.
Ivry Lighter kens the wird:

When she drops her hand, the Lights have made a spinning triple helix
in the centre of the plant. She can't hear alarms now. She only watches.
~
Darling is in the hangar when they launch, seeing how it's done.
She's thinking about telling Astrid about the boat. Will it hold her, or will
it causeforce her to go?
Darling knows which future she wants, but either way is a future. And
then Higgie's warning of the stormstrifestrainspeeddust comes. Every
Lighter knows the word:

this een coudno be warse. Sheu mynds
some aald emerjency on Mars,
some mairket crash, an whit wey her faithers
wis leukan that night: fill skaeliement,

lampan an yappan intae thir screens
whill thay thowt thay'd taen control.
But here the fock is naet o feet
an only spaek wi quiet voyces:

aa the rhythm sheu saa i'the dance,
an naen o the joy. Sheu offers tae help
an gits a piece tae stand. Sheu kens
enogh by noo tae wait an haad

this one couldn't be worse. She rememberknowreflectwills some
old emergency on Mars, some market crash, and whathowwherewhy her
fathers looked that night: total scattersmashdisorder,
    stridepacelurching and talknagbarking into their screens until they
thought they'd taken control. But here people are neat of foot and only
speak with quiet voices:
    all the rhythm she saw in the dance, and none of the joy. She offers
to help and gets a placedistancepartwhile to stand. She knows enough by
now to wait and hold

jeust whit sheu's gien tae haad, an pull
whan telt tae pull. Sheu coonts the yoles,
coonts the fock coman aff the yoles.
Sheu kens the coont gey weel the day.

An aa this time, ayont the dyke
at haads the air an separaets
the bay fae space, the Lights is hurlan
ower the yotun's faem: colour

an paitren ayont a artist's mare.
Helix, heid, matrix, mooth:
Darling pits her back tae space
an begs the coont tae come oot right.

~

only what she's given to hold, and pull when told to pull. She counts
the boats, counts the people coming off the boats. She knows the count
pretty well today.

And all this time, beyond the wallfieldbarrier that holds in the air and
separates the hangar from space, the Lights are speedthrowrolldriving over
the gas giant's foamfrothsea: colour

and pattern beyond an artist's nightmare. Helix, head, matrix, mouth:
Darling puts her back to space and begs the count to come out right.

~

Thay wirno chansan. Olaf taks
a haad o Inga's impsan, haads
tae whit is aye been shuir. But first
tae laanch means noo thir mosst deep.

Hid disno deu tae mak a coont
o whit's mistaek an whit's misanter:
thir no a puckle o meaneen atween them
whan skeel is meetan the cast o time.

The yole an hids fock deu whit they can.
An the yotun's wind an clood an Lights
is a brutal wheel birlan aa
aroon the stoor's teum ee.

~

    They weren't taking risks. Olaf holds back Inga's hurryeagerness,
holds to what has always been sure. But being first out means they are the
deepest in.

    It's no use tallying what's a mistake and what's accidentmisfortune:
there's not a grain of meaning in the difference between the two, when
skill meets the luckthrowchance of time.

    The boat and its people do what they can as the gas giant's wind and
cloud and Lights are a brutal wheel whirlrushdancespinning all around the
stormstrifestrainspeeddust's emptyhungry eye.

~

Eynar is comed tae Noor at the Hofn,
waitan in her offiece. A oor
till sheu's back, lukkan wyld
an peelie-wally. He's maed tea.

"We missed thee at the Haa," he says.
Sheu tirvs the muckle pilot glivs
an vacuum-insulaeted gansey,
taks her tea an leuks tae him.

"The Dance?" sheu says. "Oh. I'm sorry.
I lost track of the days." He shrugs.
"I doot hid's ferly busy oot here."
Sheu haals her mynd intae the reum.

Eynar has come to Noor at the Havenharbour, waiting in her office.
An hour until she gets back, looking wild and sickfeebleplain. He's made
tea.

"We missed you at the Hall," he says. She strips off the greatbig pilot
gloves and vacuum-insulated sweaterjersey, takes her tea and looks at him.

"The Dance?" she says. "Oh. I'm sorry. I lost track of the days." He
shrugs. "I expect it's veryfairly busy out here." She hauls her mind into
the room.

"Listen," sheu says, "I think I've found . . .
There's something . . . the station . . . there's something changing—"
"Yass," says Eynar, nervish. "That's why
A'm here. A'm waantan advice, fae a body—"

(the wirds is teuman oot) "—at's mibbe
traivelled a bit, so A'm here, an mibbe—"
"No," says Noor, "I mean— the Lights,
it all makes sense— the wrecks— I mean—"

But Eynar's een is coman wide.
He draps his cup. Hid hits the deck
an lands in sic a wey hid spins.
The nott o hids skuther o poly on metal

"Listen," she says, "I think I've found . . . there's something . . . the
station . . . there's something changing—" "Yes," says Eynar, nervous.
"That's why I'm here. I wantneed advice, from someone—"
(the words are pouremptying out) "—who's maybe travelled a bit, so
I'm here, and maybe—" "No," says Noor, "I mean— the Lights, it makes
sense— the wrecks— I mean—"
But Eynar's eyes are going wide. He drops his cup. It hits the deck
and lands in just such a way that it spins. The note of its skimskip of
plasticpolymer on metal

risan as it settles. Noor waits
fer the spin tae stop, an kens, an turns.
An ivry wrack ootbye is appenan.
More flooer as doar. Fractal lines

in reid an gowd spraed ower the waas
the slite plaens faaldan oot –
as gangweys? petals? Sheu sees the laefs
(trees? beuks?) wis hadden by

the maesures sheu's maed. Eynar yatters.
Sheu canno hear. Sheu's ferfil caam.
Anunder ivry laef anither.
An than inside? Noor drinks an waits.

~

rising as it settles. Noor waits for the spin to stop, and knows, and
turns. And every wreck outside is opening. More like a flower than a door.
Fractal lines
in red and gold spread over the walls, the smoothstilllevel planes
foldstrandfielding out – as gangways? petals? She sees the leaves (trees?
books?) were held by
the measures she has made. Eynar rambles. She can't hear. She's
veryfearfully calm. Beneath each leaf another. And then inside? Noor
drinks and waits.

~

Whan Darling's waitan fer the laast,
an Inga oot i'the laast is fightan
wind an tide, an Higgie an Noor
is waatchan thir unfaaldan Light,

Astrid haes the shutters doon
an cruisies slockit. Anunder her blanket,
ower thin, sheu's tryan tae haad
the pivveran pairts o hersel taegither.

This morneen sheu peyed her ticket back
fae haem tae haem, tae flit as seun
as the morn's morn, an isno telt
anither saal. Sheu disno hiv

    When Darling's waiting for the last, and Inga out in the last is
fighting wind and seatimetide, and Higgie and Noor are watching their
unfoldfielding Light,
    Astrid has the shutters down and sun-lamps turned off. Under her
blanket, too thin, she's trying to hold the shakeragethrobbing parts of
herself together.
    This morning she buypayed her ticket back from home to home, to
leaveflyescape as soon as the next morning, and she hasn't told another
soul. She doesn't have

tae gang. Hid's her fock here. Hid's Darling
here. Thir maan be a wey tae bide.
Sheu disno hiv tae gang, but that
wis the laast o her credit fae Mars i'the ticket.

Sheu's stuck hersel flittan or stuck hersel here:
yass, sheu's ferly stucken hersel
i'the sam bed sheu's gret in noo
fae sax year aald. Hid disno ken

the answer aither. Mibbe sheu'll plan
tae loup fae ship tae ship an quyt
this notion o haem, lowse hersel
intae flittan, find anither

    to go. Her people are here. Darling is here. There must be a way to
waitstaylive. She doesn't have to go, but that was the last of her credit from
Mars in the ticket.
    She's stuck leaveflyescaping or stuck here: yes, she's fairly stuck herself
in the same bed she's wept in since she was six years old. It doesn't know
    the answer either. Maybe she'll plan to jumpspringvault from ship to
ship and quit this ideaexperimentinvention of home, loosefree herself into
leaveflyescaping, find another

staetion, twatree ither planets,
a galaxy. Thinkan this
stills her skin fer a peedie while.
Sheu mynds on than that even a comet

is rived by the weyght o whit hid passes,
an whan hid's fired ootower the starns,
the starns is tirled by thir awn wheel,
an that wheel tirled in anither wheel,

til ivry escaep is anither orbit,
an ivry orbit anither still,
an ivry still aye makkan the promiese
that wi a tirl thoo'll win tae free.

station, a few other planets, a galaxy. Thinking this pauselullsecretsilences
her skin for a little while. She rememberknowreflectwills then that even a
comet
is ripbreakwrenched by the weight of what it passes, and when it's
chuckthrowfired across the stars, the stars are turntwistspinwhirled by
their own wheel, and that wheel turntwistspinwhirled in another wheel
until every escape is another orbit, and every orbit another
pauselullsecretsilence, and every pauselullsecretsilence forever making the
promise that with a turntwistspinwhirl you'll reachtravelachieve free.

Notes and Thanks

The language here is a poetic register of the Orkney tongue.
I tend towards North Isles pronunciation in my spelling, and
borrow more from the broader stream of Scots than is common
for Orkney. Alongside my own life and listening, my approach is
built on Hugh Marwick's study, *The Orkney Norn*, Gregor Lamb's
lexicon, *The Orkney Wordbook*, and grammar, *Whit Like the Day?*,
as well as the *Orkney Dictionary*, written with Margaret Flaws.
Important guides are the Orkney Sound Archive, the Orkney
Reevlers group, and the canon of Orkney language literature,
in particular C. M. Costie, Robert Rendall and Walter Traill
Dennison. The page-foot prose translation method is learned
from Robert Alan Jamieson and the combinatory translation
method from Rody Gorman. All mistakes and inconsistencies
are my own.

Versions of some poems have appeared in *Orkney Stoor*,
*Multiverse, Shoreline of Infinity, The Scores, Poetry Wales,
The Bottle Imp* and *Makar/Unmakar*.

Initial research was funded by a Creative Scotland Open Project
Fund grant, the bulk of the writing was funded by an AHRC
studentship via the Scottish Graduate School for Arts and
Humanities, and the editing was supported by a Scots Language
Publishing Grant with Stewed Rhubarb Press. The Shetland
Amenity Trust and the Sumburgh Head puffins hosted me in
a residency at a vital stage.

As supervisors, Scott Hames and Kathleen Jamie guided this book through funding, the academy, and into the world. As editors, James Harding guided the plot, Alison Miller guided the language, and Don Paterson guided the whole to publication. Salma Begum, Nicholas Blake, Laura Carr, Alice Dewing, Kieran Sangha and the whole team at Picador helped make this book much more than I'd imagined.

Gill Smee and Chris Giles gave unwavering support from the start. Conversations with Mary Blance, Leslie Burgher, Davy Cooper, Karen Esson, Bruce Eunson, Simon Hall, Donna Heddle, Laureen Johnson, Ragnhild Ljosland, Morag McInnes, Duncan McLean, Alison Miller, Nancy Scott and Roseanne Watt shaped my approach to language. Freddie Alexander, Ricky Brown, Dave Coates, Alec Finlay, Cat Fitzpatrick, Alex Fleetwood, James Harding, Elenor Holme, Robert Kiely, Evan Matyas, Karin Mckendrick, Jack McLachlan, Linden K McMahon, Christina Neuwirth, Nat Raha, Charlie Roy, Jen Stout and Alice Tarbuck read, listened, supported, encouraged and gave good notes.

Thank you to all of these people and the many more who shaped this book. And thank you again.

This beuk is dediecatid tae Darcy Leigh, freend an collaborator, pairtner an first raeder, comrade an fellow wirker, strength an joy, inspiraetion an critic, wi gratitude an love ithoot end.